Atlanta's Most Eligible Bachelor II

MIA MAE LYNNE

a "Southern Men Don't Fall In Love" novel

Published by: Book & Spirit, LLC

Cover Credit: Lex Hupertz

Edited by: Lex Hupertz

ISBN: 1943651086
ISBN-13: 978-1943651085

DEDICATION

To the almighty God of Love and Light

"Please bless this book so all readers can enjoy in the manner in which the angels and spirit guides have intended."

To my parents Johnnie Mae Parker (May 1, 1937 – April 23, 2013) and Carl Parker (April 5, 1929 – February 25, 2009)

"The lessons you gave me will follow me through eternity."

To my sons Carlos and Marcus

"Follow your dreams and the rewards will be beyond anything you can ever imagine."

To my friend Linda Smithers

"Diamonds are a girl's best friend. Your encouragement and guidance has helped me overcome seemingly impossible obstacles just by being you. You are truly my diamond."

To my friend Melissa Montgomery.

"I admire how you handle any disastrous situation with the grace and poise of the southern belle that you are. You have a gifted ability to capture the lighter side of life and spread sunshine to those who are fortunate to get to know you."

For Noel Marion, my first complete series reader

"Thank you for believing in me and taking the time to inspire me to reach for more."

For my best friend Dolphis Sloan (June 9, 1965 – February 14, 1998)

"As my big brother, you took me under your wing in my teen years and encouraged me to follow your lead in going to the University of Akron. You are a genuinely kind free spirit and even after all these years, you are still dearly missed."

ACKNOWLEDGEMENTS

"For all others who have graciously given their time to support me through the writing process, I humbly express my thanks" – Mia Mae Lynne

Kim, Dawn, Kelli & Marcella
Earth Family

Lex Hupertz
Tiffani Keaton
Mandy Varley
Nicole Westbrook
Nicole Zavodny
My Tribe

LIGHT WORKERS

"Light workers are those who are brought to earth and are unselfishly dedicated to giving their time to shine their light on humanity and make the world a better place." – Mia Mae Lynne

Debi J. Fellows
Spirals of Spirit, Painesville, Ohio

Effie Kapodistrias
Effie's Divine Celebration, Oakville, ON

Nicole Westbrook
Inner Fyre, Mentor, Ohio

Chapter 1

She was the love of his life and she'd said "Yes."

As Doug released Lisa long enough to gaze into her eyes, the anxiety of the past few weeks left him. All the questioning looks, the bewilderment, the anger, were now resolved. They were meant to be together, to share a lifetime of emotions together.

Lisa relaxed as she inhaled the last breath of Doug's kiss. She was calmer now than she had been in weeks. His unexpected proposal brought a long awaited explanation to their encounters.

Standing in the middle of a sacred space with the man she had fallen for was confirmation that they were meant to be together in holy matrimony.

Doug and Lisa realized that other people were still in the church with them. They both looked over at Rev. Morris and his wife Ikeda.

Rev. Morris gently took Ikeda's hand and walked over to Doug and Lisa. "Congratulations to the both of you and thank you for reminding me of why I married Ikeda." Rev. Morris shook Doug's hand while Doug grinned with appreciation. "We have a lot to talk about, Doug. I'll call you on Monday."

The reverend clapped Doug on the shoulder and Mrs. Morris gave Lisa a hug, and the couple walked away to give the love birds a moment alone together.

Lisa took the hand Doug offered her, let him pull her close to his body again. She inhaled the scent of his woodsy cologne. It was the one he was wearing the night of the fundraiser where they unexpectedly met again. She exhaled with her heart beating faster.

Her arms wrapped around his waist and she laid her head on his shoulder, looked up at his face turned down to hers. He smiled, and she closed her eyes, accepting the kiss he placed to her lips, a trail to her ear. "Let's go to my house."

"Okay."

Still dazed from the unexpected events of the day, they exited the church and Doug followed Lisa to her car. Lisa was enchanting in her white tea length dress that fit tightly across her waist and was flexible enough to accentuate her shapely body. He was unable to speak momentarily He never expected any woman to capture his interest or his heart in such a short time.

Lisa stopped at her car and turned to look at Doug. She gazed into his blue eyes and felt a deeper connection to him, more than she could have ever imagined. She pulled him close for another tender kiss and whispered. "I'll see you soon."

Doug parted from Lisa with his new engagement heavy on his mind.

For a commitment phobic man, he shattered his fear in less than a few months with a woman that he barely knew.

He hopped into his Mercedes and looked into his rear view mirror. Lisa was in her car ready to follow him to his home.

He took a deep breath as he drove away.

Lisa was still dazed from the turn of events this evening. She couldn't believe that she readily accepted Doug's proposal without giving it a second thought. She knew that she was in love with Doug and he was the man who would be with her for a lifetime.

Chapter 2

Lisa pulled in directly behind Doug. He was waiting for her, watching her as she came towards him. Their eyes were locked in a gentle stare. Doug opened the door, reached for her hand and they walked into house together.

Doug couldn't wait to hold Lisa in his arms again.

Feeling the desire for his new fiancée, he pressed sensual kisses against her forehead as his hands gently but firmly clasped her lower hips. His fingers squeezed her tightly and he could hear the pounding of his heart and felt a heated rush through to his core.

His lips were soft against her skin, pressing more kisses to her forehead, her jaw, down to that spot on her neck that had her head tilting back with a moan. Lisa couldn't unbutton Doug's shirt fast enough. The last few buttons popped and dropped to roll across the floor. He unzipped the back of her dress and tossed it away after she stepped out of it. Lisa jerked his belt and he assisted her with removing his pants. Off came her bra and Doug's hands rounded her hips quickly removing her panties. They both were bare, exploring each other with heated kisses.

Once Doug was fully aroused, he pulled Lisa's hand and they ran up the stairs to Doug's room. They both landed hard on the bed still squeezing, biting, sucking, and stroking, unwilling to release each other from their embrace.

Lisa parted her legs to make a cradle for Doug to fit in. He held her hip and positioned himself to enter her, thrusting hard into her body. For a moment she tensed, and he slowed, watching her face, the way her eyes slowly melted back to warm chocolate, the way her fingers moved over his back, dug into his shoulders and she smiled, matching his motions.

She wrapped her legs around his hips, shifted position so she could push him over, straddle his waist, and stare down into his surprised gaze.

Doug wrapped his hand in her hair and hauled her close to kiss her again, letting her direct their love making, enjoying the passion building between them. His eyes rolled into the back of his head and he started taking deep breaths to slow down the climax that he knew was coming.

Lisa sped up the pace. Her heart raced faster and euphoria spread through her. She climaxed, screamed and purred, falling flat on Doug's chest as she tried to catch her breath.

Doug thrust twice more, holding Lisa's hips with his own orgasm, groaning with the pleasure of his lover's body.

Her soft breasts pressed against his hairy chest. His hands wandered up and down her back, savoring the moment that froze time for their celebrated union. Doug gazed at Lisa and knew that she was the most exciting woman that he's ever had in bed.

As Doug's thoughts began to return to normal, he had a confused and dazed look. He felt a deep spiritual bond that he had never felt with a woman and was momentarily shaken to his core.

Lisa's satisfaction turned to concern. She looked at Doug and instantly knew that something was wrong. "Doug, are you okay?"

Doug gazed at Lisa and was still unable to speak. He covered her words with a deep kiss, feeling that their souls had intertwined in such a way that he knew that from now on they would never be apart. "Yes Lisa, I'm okay"

Lisa snuggled beside Doug.

They both smiled at their newfound enjoyment in exploring each other's warm hot bodies.

It was 9:00 p.m. when they woke from their light doze. The weeks of tension and the passionate love making having taken its toll on them. Now, though, they were each relaxed, with a calm peaceful glowing grin on their faces. They faced each other pleased with the fact that they would be together forever.

Lisa laughed first.

"What?" Doug asked grinning at her.

"My parents won't believe this. I've spent the last few weeks trying to convince everyone that we were just friends and no one believed me."

Doug chuckled. "I knew it was more. I just couldn't figure out why."

"Who do you want to call first?" Lisa asked.

Doug's hand caressed her arm and pulled her close. Lisa's hands gently stroked his back as he whispered in her ear.

"Let's see my Aunt Mona tonight."

"Tonight! It's late Doug. Will she be up?"

"Sure she will." Doug pulled Lisa out of the bed locking his lips against hers convincing her that it would be ok.

An hour later they arrived at Mona's door.

She was still awake and surprised to see them. "Doug, Lisa, come in. Is everything ok? Why are you here so late?" Mona stopped to observe the couple. They were smiling and holding hands. Doug's eyes twinkled and Lisa was blushing profusely.

"We just got engaged." Doug said proudly.

Mona sputtered, caught between the happy couple's hug. "Wha—When did this happen?"

"Today." Doug answered. He picked up Lisa's hand and showed his aunt the heirloom ring that she had bequeathed to him.

"Congratulations! How exciting!" She hugged both of them again and her cat peered from the kitchen to see what all of the commotion was. Mona turned around. "Shoo Whiskers."

"We're not going to stay long. We're going to stop by Lisa's parents' house before it gets too late, but we wanted you to be the first to know."

After leaving Mona's house they arrived thirty minutes later at the Dunbar home. Lights were still on because the family was entertaining relatives for the wedding of Lisa's sister, Terri, on Saturday.

Ann's eyes lit up as she embraced her daughter with a warm hug. "Lisa! I'm so glad you came by. We were just talking, Lucille and I, about—" Ann trailed off when she spotted Doug behind her daughter, only barely managing to remember her manners with her shock. "Nice to see you again, Doug. How are you doing?"

Doug shifted nervously as he grabbed Lisa's hand. He squeezed it tightly and Lisa looked up at him and smiled. His eyes twinkled as he smiled back at her. Ann's eyebrows crinkled in concern.

Lisa lifted her hand and extended it to her mother as she delivered the news.

"Doug and I just got engaged."

Ann threw her hands up and screamed.

Dave quickly jumped up from the couch and was momentarily beside his wife.

"What's going on?" Dave asked.

"Your daughter just got engaged!"

Dave grinned and offered his hand to Doug. They shook while Ann was hugging Lisa. All of them walked into the living room. Aunt Lucille heard the commotion and greeted the couple. The formal introductions were made and all sat down to talk.

"Doug, Ann is my baby sister. I flew down from Mansfield for the wedding. I'm happy for you.

What did your family say?" Lucille asked with a chuckle.

"I told my aunt today and she's ecstatic."

"What about your parents?"

Doug's face turned from merriment to a grim expression. "They passed away a long time ago."

"I'm sorry to hear that. I'm sure they would be happy for you if they were here." Ann nudged her sister, but Lucille ignored the sting, pushing Ann away to continue her inquisition. "So what do you do?"

"I work for a law firm in Atlanta."

"A lawyer? Very nice," Lucille smiled She at least knew that her niece would be taken care of. She didn't want to intrude any further, having completed her questioning anyways, and stood to leave. "It was nice meeting you, Doug. I'll see you at the rehearsal dinner tomorrow?" Lucille hugged Doug and her niece.

Lisa and Doug rose to follow Lucille from the room, knowing it was already getting late and they would be busy tomorrow.

"We have to go too. I'm off tomorrow so call me when you want me to come by," Lisa said to her mom.

The ride was a happy silence as each one was taking in their engagement announcement.

She reached for his hand to share her soul connection.

Doug looked over the center consul and smiled as he pulled his car into the garage, figuring he wasn't too tired yet, he was up for a bit more fun before the night was over.

Chapter 3

It was early dawn on Friday morning when Doug slipped out of bed, grabbed his workout gear and headed downstairs to start his routine. He had never given much thought to becoming a husband and now pondered over what exactly marriage meant.

Would he still have the freedom that he was accustomed to having?

Would he still be able to hang out with his friends?

What other changes were forthcoming?

***

Lisa felt the coldness of the sheets as she woke up in Doug's master bedroom. Missing was her new fiancé that she had tried not to fall in love with for weeks.

What made her say yes so suddenly to a man that she barely knew and yet knew all the important things about him? He was involved in personal causes, had his career, family and friends. He had a snarky sarcastic sense of humor that fit well with her spunky nature.

When Doug took the fingers of her left hand in the middle of the church, she was so startled to feel the pressure of the cold metal ring sliding towards the middle of her hand. She'd stood motionless with her thoughts so clouded that words formed at her lips but could not escape her mouth in that moment of time. That irresistible southern drawl weakened any resistance she had to push him away. Yes, was all that she could answer.

She looked over at the time on the alarm clock dreading getting out of the bed. She was aware that she didn't have a change of clothes at Doug's house and she would have to go and help her sister with her wedding.

***

Doug was still on the treadmill with his heart pounding, earphones in, listening to a pop 40 station when she appeared wearing his white button down shirt. She had on tiger bikini bottoms which showed off her cocoa brown legs. He remembered her shapely body from Miami. He almost lost count and tripped trying to turn the treadmill off.

Lisa laughed. "I didn't mean to make you lose you place, Counselor."

Doug grinned and his eyes twinkled with merriment. "I think you did."

"Maybe," she said playfully, smiling back at him.

Doug removed his sweat soaked tank top and threw it to the side. He stepped from the machine and reached for Lisa's hand, hauling her against him so he could whisper in her ear, "I'm headed to the shower, join me."

Lisa pulled him closer for a deep kiss. She rubbed his slick sweaty body and agreed with his need to shower. "Race you up the stairs!"

With that, she took off with Doug trailing her lead.

She beat him to the bathroom.

"Ladies first," Lisa reached for the nozzle and set the temperature. As the steam was rising in the bathroom, they were holding and caressing each other, removing the rest of their clothes.

Doug went first into the shower pulling Lisa in with him. "Damn, woman you like the water hot!" He quickly turned the water down while Lisa laughed.

"A little too hot for you to handle?" She asked, pressing her soft breasts into his wet hairy chest. She pulled him closer and ran her tongue up his throat, her free hand seeking other adventures at his waist.

Doug followed suit, caressing Lisa between her thighs which caused her to moan lightly. His left hand cupped her behind and her legs parted allowing him to feel inside her honey pot. Lisa's moans came faster and louder as Doug teased inside her feminine walls.

Doug's cock stood at attention as he turned her to face the wall. He raised her hands over her head and she leaned against her bent arms, letting him take control while he stroked over her breasts, down her toned belly, cupped her buttocks to cant her hips further back, easing his entry into her tight sheath from behind.

She moaned when he pressed into her.

He bit her neck to bite back his answering sound.

With Lisa's hands firmly pressed against the shower wall she pushed her hips back to receive all of Doug. They both rocked in a rhythmic motion enjoying the connection of oneness that they shared. The bathroom was full of steam and the beads of water continued to pound on their bodies as they enjoyed the pleasure of each other.

Lisa reached her peak first, Doug followed.

He let out a loud groan. "I'm coming, Lisa"

Both of their hearts were beating rapidly. Lisa turned around and Doug cupped her butt as he pulled her close in his arms again. They stared at each other as they were gasping for air. Both stood there, relishing in the kisses they shared.

Doug said, "I'm calling off work."

Lisa looked into Doug's blue eyes and watched the water stream from his forehead down through the shadows of the lightly forming beard and moustache.

"I like the grizzled look on you. Makes you more dashing."

"I'll grow it out for you."

"I can't wait to feel it." Doug laughed.

"I hate to break the mood but I have to help my sister with the wedding so I can't stay long."

"Ok, let's finish up. I'm sure you have a lot to do."

Chapter 4

Lisa stopped by her sister's apartment early in the morning before going to her aunt's house. She knocked on the door and Terri answered, still in her pajamas.

"Come in baby sister. I hear you have news." She hugged Lisa tightly, pulling her inside the apartment.

"Doug and I are getting married. Who told you?"

"Mom told me that. No way! I knew you were in love with him. Tell me how he proposed. I want all the details! "

Lisa filled her sister in on all of the events of the night before. He sister's eyes widened at the story.

Terri held up a hand stopping Lisa's story. "Wait, stop. This is too good to rush and I have way too much to do today to get all the good stuff...but—"

Lisa groaned, having already planned on accompanying Terri to her events but acting sisterly in complaining anyways, unable to keep up the act and laughing at the waggle of her sister's eyebrows.

Lisa slapped her sister playfully, "Don't ever do that again."

Terri waggled her eyebrows again and then stopped to beg Lisa. "Come with me. I have to get my hair and nails done and you can get yours done too and tell me the rest."

Lisa laughed again, catching Terri's hand with a squeeze before rising, already late to her meeting. "I can't. I have to help Aunt Olivia out with the dinner for the reception. You know we have a large family."

"Stacy and Maya will be there and Auntie O knows lots of people. She won't miss you. Plus," Terri put her hands on her hips and struck a haughty pose, "I'm the bride. You have to cater to me."

Lisa laughed. "Call me when you're getting your nails done and I may swing by."

Lisa left and arrived at her aunt's house.

She was really excited about her engagement and knew the gossip through the family was already brewing. She didn't want to take away from her sister's wedding day, but she had joyful news of her own that she wanted to share.

Maya opened the door before Lisa could knock. She gave Lisa a big bear hug. "I heard you got engaged. Congratulations!"

"Thank you." Lisa knew that her family spread gossip faster than a wildfire. She brought her groceries to the kitchen and set down her belongings, washed her hands and proceeded to the table to help chop the carrots.

Her aunt and Stacy greeted her with warm smiles.

"I heard the news. Congratulations." Stacy said as she hugged Lisa.

Aunt Olivia continued to mix the batter for the muffins that she was making for the reception. Lisa walked over and kissed her on the cheek. Aunt Olivia leaned over to receive the affection and gave her a disapproving look. Lisa smiled. She was prepared for the battle.

"A white boy? What are you going to do if he calls you a monkey to your face? I don't have bail money for you."

The cousins smirked and turned away. They wanted no part of this discussion.

"It won't happen. You won't have to worry about bail money. He's not like that."

"They are all like that. If he's not like that then where has he been hiding? Southern white man. They are all like that. That's all they know." Olivia shook her head and continued to make her cornbread. "Lisa, you've only known this man a short time. Have you thought this over? Does he know what he's doing?" Olivia folded her arms with a scowl on her face.

Lisa was taught to respect her elders and this was becoming a challenge. Her Aunt O was one who always was vocal about her opinions no matter if they were right or wrong. Lisa was not going to battle her aunt but was not going to be bullied by her either.

"Auntie, we're going to have a long engagement. We'll have plenty of time to discuss everything, including racial matters."

"Well, you were always one to do whatever you wanted. Don't let that white man run you. You know I don't like this."

Lisa nodded and acknowledged her aunt's statement. Her aunt had a personal history with white men and had no love lost for them. Olivia suffered through the Jim Crow era and was an activist against her mother's wishes. She still had emotional and physical scars from participating in the protest marches in the sixties.

"I know Auntie, I won't let Doug do that to me. Everything is different now. It's not the same as when you and mom grew up."

"It's the same. Get your head out of the sand and read the papers. The KKK still marches, black men and women are still getting killed by the police for no reason. It's still the same. Covert versus overt. Watch him."

Lisa knew that she wouldn't win this argument with her aunt. She desperately wanted to tell her to bug off but that wasn't good family politics.

Stacy said, "I've got to see the ring."

Lisa raised her hand to show everyone her ring.

Her Aunt Olivia was not impressed. "That's awfully small."

Lisa couldn't keep the bite out of her voice as she responded to her aunt's comment. "It's his grandmother's ring."

"He couldn't buy you his own ring?" Olivia snorted.

"It's so romantic Auntie O" Maya said. "Don't you wish you had your grandmother's ring?"

"I suppose so but it's gonna be trouble marrying that white boy. I know his family don't like it. What happened with him? Did Atlanta run outta white women to date? He got jungle fever or something?" Olivia chuckled at her own joke.

"Mom!" Stacy shouted. "Can't you just be happy for Lisa?"

"I am. Can't wait to meet him. Are you bringing him to the wedding?"

"Yes and leave him alone."

She continued to help prepare the meal for a while and made her excuses to leave, claiming Terri needed her, which was true, mostly. Besides, she could do without the wallowing. She wanted to be happy with the new stage of her relationship.

***

Doug told Lisa that he would meet her for a late lunch when she went to help her aunt that morning. He suddenly realized that the only person among his family and friends that knew about his engagement was his Aunt Mona. It was about 9:00 a.m. when he called his friend, Greg, at the office.

"What's up Doug? Are we hanging out tonight? I hadn't heard from you in a minute."

"I got engaged to Lisa last night."

Greg howled through the phone, "Get the fuck outta here? You're lying! Congratulations man. It was a matter of time. What did her family say?"

"They were fine with it."

"What made you do it? If I ever got engaged, my mom would throw a party. She's already pressing me for grandkids." Greg chuckled with his statement.

"It was a matter of time. I really missed her this week. Let's have drinks soon. This is a busy weekend."

"Now that you're engaged, is she going to let you out?" Greg asked teasingly.

"I sure hope so or I won't be engaged long," Doug said emphatically. "I still need my freedom and so does she."

"I get that, man…shit. Look Doug, I've got to go. I've got a meeting in about fifteen minutes. I'll talk to you next week. Congratulations again."

"Thanks, Greg. Talk to you then."

Doug hung up with his friend and decided to call a few more of his relatives and friends to give them the news. He called Lisa and they agreed on where to meet for a late lunch. They picked a local sandwich place because Lisa didn't have a lot of time between the cooking and meeting Terri for her nails.

***

Marietta Diner was one of the best restaurants in the city. Doug knew the owner and had no problem getting a table. After they ordered with the waitress, Lisa reached across the table to hold Doug's hand. She could feel the gentle strength as his hands clasped into hers. She looked at the details of his fingernails and the pale shade of his skin against her dark complexion. She gazed back up into his eyes. "Doug, I still can't believe we got engaged last night. We still have a lot to learn about each other. I still value my freedom."

Doug grinned as he released her hand to grab the napkin from the table and wipe his mouth before speaking. "I was thinking about that today actually. We can work through the freedom part."

"I'm sure we can Doug. I still have soccer practice, nights out with my girlfriends, social events... But we still have to make time for each other too."

"We will. Don't worry Lisa, it will work out. Let's not stress over it. The reason that it will work is because we have separate activities."

Lisa frowned, "That's not reassuring Doug. It sounds like we will be passing each other in the night. That's not what marriage is about."

Doug took notice of Lisa's unhappiness and tried to smooth things over. "No Lisa, I'm not advocating separate lives. Some of the divorce's

I've seen are because the partners don't have separate activities. We'll have lots of activities together."

"Ok, I think I get what you are saying. Wife complains that husband comes home and sits on the couch. Husband complains that wife is too busy, like in my case, I have soccer parents that are always running to soccer fields, and they don't have time for each other."

"Lisa, I know that soccer is important to you. I will come to some of your games or practices when it works for both of us. Just like reading time at the library and my personal social causes are important to me. I don't expect you to participate in all of my causes, but I'm not giving them up either."

Lisa acknowledged his thoughtful response. They were going to be a couple but a very busy couple with their own personal interests. They would have plenty of time during the engagement to see how everything would work out.

Chapter 5

Doug gave Lisa a kiss and walked her to her car, waved as she left to help her sister and he returned home to make phone calls for work. The rehearsal dinner was at 6:00 p.m. and he would meet Lisa there later. He sat down on the couch, picked up the Wall Street Journal and chuckled to himself. Since the plane trip from Miami where Lisa plopped down in the seat next to him, he recalled that memory every time he read the paper. He settled in to read a few stories on the market.

A little while later he found himself napping and woke up in the early evening. He didn't realize how tired he was from the events overnight and even the past week. He looked at his watch and realized that time had passed him by.

"Oh, shit! I overslept and have to hurry to get ready."

Doug arrived at the church parking the same time as the wedding party. He slipped in quietly through the side of the church and slid into one of the back pews. He gazed down the aisle and there she was, standing among the other bridesmaids, dressed in casual clothes. He waved, catching her gaze and she smiled and winked at him acknowledging his presence.

Doug always knew that if he ever got married that he wanted a big wedding. His parents were gone but he had a lot of friends and family that would love to see him happy. He was only getting married once. Lisa was his true love and he wanted the world to see them together.

***

When Lisa spotted Doug walking into the church, she imagined what it would be like to marry Doug on a beach on a tropical island. She could wear a sundress and he could wear khaki's, sandals and a light cotton shirt. The sun would bleach his golden locks and the wind would be swift enough to cool their bodies from the heat. They could spend their nights dining and dancing on the beach just like their time spent in Miami but longer.

Her sister interrupted her thoughts. "Lisa, did you tell Aunt O that I wanted a tray of her special fudge to take with me on my honeymoon."

"I did. I've got it in the car. I'll run and get it." Lisa quickly dashed out to the car to bring in the special tin for her sister. The two briefly talked and Lisa returned to standing in front of the church with the bridesmaids. The rehearsal was over fifteen minutes later and everyone went downstairs to a classroom where food was being served buffet style. Lisa waited until everyone left before sitting down next to Doug. "Are you hungry?"

"Sure."

She smiled and gave him a brief peck on the cheek. "Let's go eat."

***

Doug and Lisa entered the classroom and grabbed their plates. The food was catered from a local soul food restaurant. After making their selections, they sat at the only table with any seats left. Doug sat next to an African-American man who had black curly locks and was gazing down at his food. He looked up when Doug sat down.

"I'm Doug Bader, Lisa's fiancé."

"I'm Carter Glass." He extended his hand with a warm and friendly grip which Doug returned firmly.

"Are you related to Lisa?"

Carter grinned, "Naw, I'm friends with Terri and Ricky. Congratulations on your engagement, by the way. You guys set a date yet?"

Doug laughed, "No, we got engaged last night."

Carter said in a serious tone. "It's good that you made your move. I moved too late and lost out. If she's the one, make sure you keep her happy."

Doug thoughtfully took in each of Carter's strong words of advice. "I couldn't agree with you more, Carter." He reached under the table and took Lisa's hand.

She stopped her conversation, turned, and smiled at him. Doug gazed back into Lisa's dark brown eyes and felt a warm rush of emotions running from the tip of his fingers through his entire body. Lisa was his and let no one come between them.

Doug's natural closeness to Lisa was suddenly interrupted by a call to nature. He excused himself and found the restroom. Afterwards, he stood outside of the church to take a call when he heard angry shouting coming from a car with the windows open. It was Terri and her fiancé.

"Why the hell are you having a bachelor party tonight? You and I both have all this family here and a big day tomorrow. Are you trying to ruin it on purpose?"

"Hell naw, Terri. Tony just got here and I haven't seen him in a minute. We won't stay out long."

"You'll ruin the pictures hung over with bloodshot eyes. Where are you going? A strip club."

Ricky was irritated and looked out of the windshield and saw that Doug was not very far away. He got out of the car and turned his anger towards him.

"What the hell are you listening to, cracker?"

Doug didn't respond. His jaw tightened, his shoulders squared and he looked Ricky directly in the eye.

Terri watched both of the men, got out of the car, and confronted Ricky. "Don't change the subject. Doug's got nothing to do with this. Leave him out of this." She turned to Doug. "Just go. This isn't your business."

"You sure, Terri?" Doug didn't take his eyes off the angry black man.

"I said go, Doug."

He nodded and walked back into the church trying to control his temper that was at the breaking point. He returned to the table and sat beside Lisa.

"What is it, Doug?"

It took Doug a moment to compose himself. He picked up Lisa's hand and held it firmly in his lap. He drew a big breath and answered. "Nothing, Lisa."

Just as he answered, the quarrelling couple returned from the parking lot. Terri looked stressed and Ricky full of anger. Ricky glared at Doug and Doug returned the stare. Doug held Lisa's hand tighter and kissed her softly behind her ear.

"I have a few things to take care of. I'll see you at home later."

"What" Lisa said, "I thought I had you to myself this evening." Doug sighed and relaxed with her statement.

"You do. Come with me."

"Doug! You know that I have a lot to do." As Lisa said her statement, she rethought her previous answer. "I'll be home in an hour."

Doug kissed her cheek again and quietly left the church.

Chapter 6

Lisa woke up the next morning with her sandy blonde Adonis next to her. He was still asleep with a peaceful grin on his face. She took her fingers and lightly traced his arm starting from his wrist all the way up to his shoulders. The fine curly hairs on his arms were springing back with each stroke of her hand.

She nestled in closer pressing her breasts to his back. She stroked his finely tuned body and hairy chest. Chest hair was very sexy, she smiled to herself. Especially on Doug. Nice package. If this was the man she would be waking up with every morning for the rest of her life, then "yes" was the right answer.

Doug was usually an early riser. This morning he wanted to have time with Lisa. Waking up with her by his side was an unanticipated and yet rewarding outcome of a brief courtship that was really designed by fate.

His engagement to Lisa was heavy on his mind. He didn't anticipate the antagonistic response from Ricky as well as the quizzical looks, hush-hush chatter and outright blatant questions about himself. He never believed that color would be an issue between them but didn't know that it could be a problem for others.

As he came out of his deep conscious thought, he felt Lisa exploring his family jewels. He was fully awake.

"Breakfast in bed?" he joked.

Lisa laughed: "I thought you'd never ask."

For the next hour they played with each other on an intimate level. The cares, concerns and worries were gone. Their passion peaked and each one was once again in each other's arms. Doug broke the calm and peaceful moment. "I want you to move in next weekend."

Lisa was startled. She felt the sincerity in his statement. They just got engaged a couple of days ago and she hadn't given it a second thought. She knew that it would take some time to get to know each other better but moving in now would be much different than a temporary arrangement. She would be here for a lifetime.

"That's pretty soon Doug. We tried that before."

"And I still didn't get my entire week. The holidays are coming up. I want you here with me before then."

"Well counselor, you waste no time. Tell me do you always move this quickly or is it because of me."

Doug laughed. "It's because of you. I normally don't move at all or break things off. What's your answer?"

"Doug, I don't like being pressured into anything."

"I'm not pressuring you"

"Yes You Are" Lisa said emphatically.

"Ok, I'll move in your place and we can stay there."

"That's ridiculous! Your belongings won't fit into my apartment." Doug smiled and Lisa knew that she'd been had.

"I'll think about it this week and give you an answer. I want to get through my sister's wedding first. Too many big decisions at one time."

***

Lisa and Doug arrived later that morning for Terri and Ricky's wedding. Doug took a seat on a pew on the bride's side of the aisle with the family. He noticed that most of the well-wishers for both the bride and groom were mainly African-American. He never really noticed in his daily activities that he was in a majority culture. He never gave it a second thought. Is this how life with

34

Lisa will be in the future? Two very distinct and different cultures.

The music started and the wedding ceremony began. There was a mixture of the traditional wedding music and some songs that he never heard before. He looked across the aisle and Lisa appeared. She was her sister's maid of honor and exquisite in her pink satin and lace attire. Lisa was strikingly beautiful walking down the aisle taking part in this very sacred ceremony.

Terri came down the aisle with her father. She was smiling and glowing as a beautiful bride should be. It was much different than the stressed out bride bickering with her soon to be husband. Even Ricky looked happy when he saw Terri come down the aisle. Maybe this couple will last through their difficulties.

***

The wedding reception began. Lisa sat at the bridal table which left Doug to sit with his future father-in-law Dave and Dave's brother Ray. Ray was very friendly and shook Doug's hand while Dave introduced them. They began conversing and realized that they had some common connections.

The music began to slow down. Doug gazed over to Lisa and she excused herself from the table. Doug outreached his hand to take her to the dance floor. He slowly led her in a side to side motion capturing the rhythm as his beauty was held securely and closely to him. Lisa was so enrapt in the dance that she momentarily forgot she was at her sister's wedding reception.

Lisa whispered to Doug. "Nice moves counselor. How long do you want to stay?"

"As long as you want Lisa. No hurry for me"

"Next weekend is fine with me."

Doug stopped their dance and gazed into her eyes. "I said no pressure Lisa."

"I'm ready Doug." Lisa pressed her lips against Doug's cheek and he turned to delicately kiss her soft succulent lips. The song ended and began a new tune. By this time Lisa's parents were watching them as well as a few others. Lisa didn't intend to take the attention away from the bride but somehow managed to do so. Lisa's mother Ann came to Lisa's side.

"We have a few more pictures to take and then if you and Doug want to get out of here, then go."

Lisa nodded and Doug never took his eyes off her while her mother was talking. She gave Doug a quick kiss and followed her mother away. Doug adjusted his jacket and straightened his tie before returning to mingle with the guests.

Carter approached him and he extended his hand, happy to see the man he'd spoken to at the rehearsal here for the night.

"You're in pretty deep."

Doug let his gaze find Lisa in the crowded room. "I am."

"Make sure it stays that way and don't let her out of your sight."

Doug nodded in agreement, clapping the man's shoulder as Lisa returned and they bid walked away to bid farewell to the newly married couple.

Chapter 7

Two weeks later, as Doug prepared to leave for work, Lisa was slow to rise. She had been up all night in the bathroom sick to her stomach. She didn't want Doug to worry so she let him sleep peacefully unaware of her troubles. She called the office informing them that she wouldn't be in that day and got back into bed once Doug left.

"This virus better go away soon," she said to herself.

She forgot her lunch appointment with Doug and was soon fast asleep.

**

Doug arrived at Lisa's office and Mona greeted her nephew.

"Have you seen Lisa this morning? We're supposed to have lunch."

"She called in sick. Didn't she tell you?" Mona asked.

Doug's face turned a pale ashen white. He thought back to the night of their engagement. Their connection to each other was deeper than he ever imagined.

"No. She did say anything. I have to go home and check on her." Doug left his aunt, rushed to the drugstore and made his purchase. He sped home to see her.

"Lisa, Lisa!" he called out as he entered the house.

When she didn't answer, he headed upstairs to their bedroom, wondering if she was still asleep and if she was still feeling unwell. He found her in their bed and stared for a moment, glancing down her sleeping body to her stomach hidden beneath the covers.

He sat down on the bed next to her, gently shaking her arm to wake her.

Startled, she looked first at him and then at the clock. "I didn't know it was so late. I'm sorry I missed our lunch. I should have told you I wasn't feeling well."

Doug looked Lisa over. Oh yes. It was true.

"We had a lunch date and when you weren't at the office, I came home to see if you were ok."

Lisa sat up and rubbed her eyes. She was fully awake "I think I have a virus. I didn't want to worry you. I was up all night with it."

Doug leaned over and kissed her forehead still clutching the package in his hand. "Lisa, you have more than a virus."

Doug handed Lisa the package from the drugstore. She pulled out the contents and was surprised at what she found. "A pregnancy test!" She exclaimed. "Are you serious?"

"Oh yes. You're pregnant."

"But…how? When?"

"The night we got engaged."

"What?"

"Lisa—I, we didn't use protection or take any precautions. Just, take the test, okay?" Doug's face was grim as he looked her in the eyes.

"Doug—"

"Please," His expression softened. "Please, just take the test for me."

Lisa hesitated but couldn't deny the look in Doug's eyes. "Okay."

Lisa entered the bathroom, her thoughts running fast through her head.

Yes, she was late.

No, she wasn't on birth control.

Maybe, Doug could be right.

Shit.

She hesitated before moving to the toilet. How did someone take one of these tests anyways? Could it be any more awkward?

"How's it coming?

"Fine, Doug."

She took a deep breath, read the instructions and closed her eyes tight. Not wanting to watch as she took the test and waited the time for the reading to appear.

As the test started to turn pink, she screamed in the bathroom.

Doug rushed to the door. "Lisa, are you okay?"

Doug opened the bathroom door. Lisa's hand was clenching the test strip and she was breathing fast as she stared at it in disbelief. She didn't even look up at him when he knelt at her side, and pulled the small, pink tipped strip from her grip.

Doug started to grin, "Yes ma'am, you're pregnant. It looks like we have to move the wedding up."

Lisa couldn't believe she was going to be a mother, let alone think about that in terms of getting married too.

She looked at Doug's elated expression and wondered how he was so excited about this since it was terrifying her. She wondered how he'd known in the first place.

He hugged her, pulled her tightly to him with a happy laugh that she couldn't return, not yet, at least. "Let's get you back to bed!"

She was reeling.

Two months ago she started a new job. Then she'd met her future husband, and now was going to be a mother.

How much change could she possibly take in such a short period of time?

Lisa sat up, embraced Doug, and whispered in his ear. "I love you."

"I love you too, Lisa."

Doug helped Lisa to lie back down and get some more rest, told her he was just going to go out into the hallway for a minute but would be right back.

He closed the door softly behind him, leaned against the heavy wood with a smile.

Becoming a father confirmed his suspicion of what happened during the night of their engagement. He didn't want to scare Lisa with his prediction of her pregnancy. He stared at Lisa hoping that she would be okay with her pregnancy news. Doug kissed Lisa on the forehead and left her to rest. He went to his den and called his Aunt Mona with the good news.

"Grant & Company CPA's, Linda speaking. How may I assist you?"

"This is Doug Bader. May I speak to my Aunt Mona, please?"

"Just a moment, let me see if she's available."

Doug waited through the silence pacing nervously back and forth.

The phone clicked back from hold. "Hi Doug."

"I just talked to Lisa."

"Is she okay?"

"Yes ma'am, she'll be fine. She doesn't have a virus."

"She doesn't?"

"No ma'am…she has morning sickness."

Doug heard the phone drop. He wasn't sure what happened to her. "Aunt Mona, are you still there? Is everything okay?"

"Sorry, I was just shocked. Are you sure she's pregnant?"

Doug laughed, "Oh definitely. I was there when it happened." Doug rubbed the back of his head to calm his excitement. "We're trying to get her into the doctor's office tomorrow so she won't be in. It looks like you are going to be a great aunt again!"

Doug chatted with Aunt Mona for a few more minutes before finally finding the chamomile tea and setting the kettle to boil. He hung up and looked in his fridge to see what he could prepare for his pregnant fiancée. Pregnant. He shook his head, still experiencing the high of the news.

He thought back over the last few weeks. Fate had determined that he would become a husband and a father. With Lisa by his side, he was ready to accept the responsibility.

Doug returned to the bedroom with the tea.

Lisa sat up and drank the tea. As it started to digest, she began to feel a little better, and with feeling better came the questions she couldn't help be ask. "What am I going to tell my parents?" She'd just gotten engaged. She wasn't expecting to become a mother.

"We'll take it one step at a time, Lisa. I'm with you all the way."

"Doug, my life is changing so fast. I started a new job, met you, got engaged, and now I'm going to be a mother. All of this in the last eight weeks!"

Doug laughed at her expression. He hugged her, shifting so he could sit next to her on the bed and wrap his arm behind her back, pull her into his side.

"I've had drastic changes as well. Two months ago I was the most eligible bachelor in Atlanta. Then I met you, got engaged and now I'm going to be a father in those same eight weeks you mentioned."

Lisa started laughing. "Oh my God." It was either laugh or cry, and she had to keep reminding herself that Doug was with her in this. "Let's call my parents later and see if they can come over. We'll think of something to say before then."

Chapter 8

The doorbell rang and Doug answered with a smile on his face. "Hello Ann. Hi Dave. Welcome to our home."

Ann gave Doug a warm hug and Dave shook his hand. Doug led Ann and Dave to the dining area and Lisa came out of the kitchen.

"Hi Mom and Dad, dinner will be ready soon."

Ann asked, "Do you want me to help with anything?"

"Doug's got it. Thanks Mom." Doug followed Lisa back to the kitchen and proceeded to help her. Lisa turned to face Doug. "What are we going to say? Do I just blurt out I'm pregnant or do we discuss the wedding plans first?"

"Let's discuss the plans first. If they ask why so soon, then we can tell them."

"We should tell them anyway."

"Good point, Lisa. I'll let you take the lead."

Lisa gave Doug a kiss and he flashed her his sexy boyish grin. He knew that tonight would be a difficult conversation with her parents especially since everyone was still adjusting to their quick romance. Doug grabbed the heavier of the dishes and followed Lisa to the dining room.

Lisa paused for a moment looking Doug directly in his eyes. She couldn't believe how fast she had become attached to a man that she didn't know very well. She grabbed the sausage rolls she'd made for an appetizer and headed for her parents with a deep breath.

***

Ann noticed that Doug and Lisa both looked just as nervous as the first evening that Lisa brought him by.

Lisa twirled her fork through the spaghetti and never picked it up.

Doug gulped down his third Vodka tonic. The quick disappearance of the alcohol caused Ann concern.

She hoped that Lisa wasn't engaged to an alcoholic. She watched Doug and Lisa have an unspoken conversation between them, the way their eyes met and heads shook and darted away again. Ann looked at Dave to see if he could read into what was going on between the two.

She broke the silence.

"Have you two set a date?"

Doug blurted out. "Yes ma'am, early February."

Lisa looked over at Doug continuing the silent conversation between the two of them. He spoke too soon. Doug looked at Lisa and shrugged as if there was nothing wrong with his statement.

"That's kind of soon. Do you plan to have a big wedding or a small wedding?" Dave asked.

Lisa answered "Small" and Doug answered "Big." They both stared at each other.

Ann said, "It doesn't look like you've discussed it much. If you want a big wedding, three months is not enough time to plan. Those weddings take almost a year."

Doug blurted out again. "We can't wait that long."

Lisa nudged Doug under the table.

"Why is that, Doug?" Ann asked. Her curiosity was heightened by the sudden interest to rush this marriage. She was anticipating the next response.

"I'm pregnant Mom. I just found out this morning."

Ann and Dave shouted together, "Pregnant!"

"How long ago did this happen?" Ann asked.

"What do you mean pregnant?" Dave growled.

"We think when we got engaged." Lisa answered.

Doug continued, "So we want to have the wedding soon."

Lisa added, "If it's past mid-February, we might as well get married at the courthouse."

Ann said, "Terri and I will plan the wedding. We'll have it in February. Doug, Lisa, I've never seen anything move faster than the two of you. You went from acquaintances to roommates to fiancées to parents all in the last four weeks. Now we are planning a rapid pace wedding. I certainly hope this marriage lasts longer than this romance."

Doug interjected. "Lisa and I can handle this."

"No," Ann shouted. "My daughter has too much going on and now she's pregnant.

"Mom, it's our wedding and Doug and I will plan this."

Dave said, "Listen to your mother. There is a lot to do in planning a wedding. You don't have time to do this by yourself."

Lisa reflected on her dad's words. She knew that taking care of herself would be the number one priority. She had a full time job and coached a soccer team. Maybe it wouldn't be bad if her Mom and sister helped.

"You and Terri can plan it but Doug and I make all the final decisions."

Lisa felt Doug's hand clasp hers under the table. She glanced over at his noncommittal expression.

"We'll do whatever Lisa wants." Doug said in a matter of fact tone. Lisa squeezed his hand and Doug drew a breath and exhaled to release some tension.

Dave directed his question to Doug. "Do you have anything else to tell us?"

"I don't know what else to say." Doug answered. "Lisa and I were reflecting on all of the changes in the past eight weeks this morning."

Dave folded his napkin on the table, leaning back in his chair to look at his daughter and soon to be son-in-law, "So I'm getting my first grandchild."

Lisa smiled but the expression was more tense than happy. Still unsure of what to make of everything that was happening to her. "In about nine months."

Chapter 9

It was the first chance Doug had been able to schedule Lisa in for an appointment with the physician. They arrived at the doctor's office early Tuesday morning. The place was crowded with women at various stages of pregnancy. As Lisa and Doug took a seat in the waiting room, he offered her a magazine. He purposely picked up the one showing a woman in her third trimester. He flashed her a grin.

"Why are you smiling?" Lisa asked.

"Are you ready to be parents?" Doug asked, still grinning.

Lisa could tell that Doug was more than ready to start a family. Before she could ask him any more questions, the nurse called her name to come back to the patient room and Doug waited until he was needed.

While in the office, she took another pregnancy test and all was confirmed. After the appointment was completed, Lisa's doctor consulted with her and Doug in his office regarding the news.

Doug had a lot of questions and used numerous medical terms.

Lisa thought they were talking a foreign language and couldn't wait to get out of the office.

Finally, the visit ended.

As they walked away from the doctor's office, Doug's excitement couldn't be contained. "There's a schedule that you will need to follow as far as diet and exercise. There's an abundance of materials on pregnancy. I have some old medical books and there's a ton of information online."

Lisa was unable to connect to his conversation as she was still reeling from the news. "I'm having information overload. Please give me a breather on this for a minute."

"No way, this is my baby. Don't worry. I'll plan this out for you and make it simple."

Lisa's stomach started growling, and it wasn't just from hunger. She was becoming annoyed with his overbearing behavior. His excitement was too much for her to handle right now. What was she going to do with a baby? She just started her accounting career, got engaged and now she's pregnant. She felt Doug's enthusiasm as he hugged her again giving her several kisses. Each kiss eased her concerns and she finally laughed. Maybe this won't be so bad. "Okay Doug, can we please eat now? I'm hungry."

"Ok but I will assist you in what you should eat." Doug knew Lisa wasn't handling the unexpected pregnancy well. He wanted to make sure she and the baby were healthy. He wrapped her in his arms hoping she would relax and enjoy becoming a mother.

Doug was smothering her with his emotions. She didn't hear anything else that he said, only realized that it was getting late in the day and she had things to do and needed a break from her fiancé. "Don't you have to go back to work?"

"After we eat I'll go to the office late afternoon."

She smiled and hoped he bought the expression, hoped she could make it through lunch if he was going to continue acting this way.

Doug selected an Italian restaurant and arranged for them to sit in a quiet booth near the kitchen. He was courteous and took her coat for her and Lisa thought about forgiving him for his attitude and over bearing nature. He was probably just as nervous as she was, and he did have more of a background in pregnancy than her, what with almost being a doctor and all. She could listen to him, humor him, for a while.

They discussed menu options, but when Doug suggested a modification to her selection, Lisa couldn't take it anymore. "Are you going to be doing this for nine months?"

Doug was a little embarrassed. He wasn't sure of how to answer her question without sparking her anger. But he knew what he was talking about. He knew this stuff. He still needed to be in control. "Yes."

"Why?" Lisa threw her hands up in the air, leaned away from the table like she was contemplating leaving.

Doug could see the fire in her eyes. She sat up straight in her chair and gave him an icy stare.

He didn't want Lisa to make a scene and wanted her to eat. He tried to smooth it over. "Lisa, I love you. When I said that I was ready to commit to you, I meant it. That commitment is also to your health, as well as our baby's. I want you to be with me for a very long time."

Lisa wasn't sure how to respond to his affirmation. She restrained herself from starting an argument in the middle of the restaurant by digesting each and every word he said. She was sure that he conned her with his smooth response but she accepted his expression of love. "I love you too, Doug." She said with a plastered smile on her face. Doug didn't seem to realize how fake it was.

She let him order for her anyways.

***

After lunch, Doug dropped Lisa off at home and went to his office. His secretary, Rebecca, greeted him with a few messages and his revised calendar of events to take place in the afternoon.

Doug thanked her and retreated to his office to call his associate Harold into his office.

"What's up, Doug?"

"Can you meet me and Greg for drinks at Dupree Country Club this evening?"

"Sure, why?"

"I want to discuss my wedding plans."

Harold left Doug's office, he had a moment to call Greg and invite him to dinner this evening.

All of the men arrived at the restaurant together. They ordered appetizers and drinks and started talking about the local sports team. But this wasn't about sports, and both Greg and Harold knew the Lisa and Doug's wedding was the biggest thing on Doug's mind.

Greg asked, "Doug, What's up? You called me to come and discuss wedding plans? Are you getting married soon? You just got engaged."

"The wedding is in February."

"Why? Is she pregnant?"

Doug gave Greg a silent response.

Greg realized that he guessed the big news. "Aw hell nah? You just got engaged and you got her pregnant already?"

Harold asked, "Is she really pregnant?"

Doug sat back in his chair and a big smile started to widen across his face. Doug loved little kids and never expected to have one of his own. Although Lisa's pregnancy was unexpected, the timing couldn't have been better and she was the woman who he wanted to have them with. "Oh definitely, I know exactly when it happened." Doug said in a smug and confident voice.

Greg shook his head and laughed at Doug's expression. His bachelor friend was now going to have a wife and family. "You don't waste any time. So you're getting married in February?"

Doug answered, "Yes, I want both of you in my wedding. I called my brother Todd and cousin Bruce to be in it too."

Harold said, "Yes sir, I wouldn't miss it."

Greg added in, "I'll be there too, and I'll even throw the bachelor party."

Harold teased Doug. "Well Doug, it looks like it's too late for the vasectomy you were considering."

Doug laughed, "Lisa can have as many of my kids as she wants."

Greg and Harold laughed with him. Greg and Doug looked across the restaurant and saw a woman that they both knew. Katie was a co-worker of Greg's and an old flame of Doug's.

"Hello gentlemen. What's new?" Katie said.

Doug was still laughing as Katie came to the table. He had enjoyed their casual dating but she'd been too much maintenance for him to keep up with. She required a man with a lot of cash and he wasn't willing to be her banker. She always looked good on his arm for a business or social affair.

Doug gave Katie his engagement news. She was standing at the time and Greg motioned for her to take a seat in the extra chair at the table. Katie asked a few questions and Doug was happy to answer. A few minutes later Katie excused herself from the table. She told the group that she had personal errands to run and would see them another time.

Greg watched her go. "That's another one that's mad you are getting married. Do you know how many women are GOING TO BE upset over this?"

"I only care if Lisa is upset. I don't want or need the rest of them."

"You are in this pretty deep Doug. I promise, I am really happy for you, but how are you going to handle all the problems of a mixed-race couple?" Greg asked.

Doug looked at Greg curious about his question. The thought hadn't crossed his mind about an interracial relationship. Lisa was everything he had ever wanted in a woman. She accepted his quirky personality and adapted to it. The more time they spent together the more he were sure they were meant to be together. Having deep conversations about race wasn't an important topic. But maybe it should be. "Lisa and I haven't discussed it."

Greg was amazed. "You haven't? You're going to marry her. You're having kids with her. And you haven't discussed being a mixed-race couple? You have to discuss it! It won't go away."

Harold added, "Greg's right. There have been some ugly comments at the office that no one would dare say to your face. There are people out there that won't and don't accept this."

Doug looked from one man to the other, with worry on his face. Were they right? "It hasn't come up yet. I think that had Lisa and I met under normal circumstances, we would have discussed this up front. We will have our opportunity to talk about it."

Harold said, "I don't want you or Lisa to be hurt by these comments. These people have very narrow minds. Both of you must be on solid ground with each other on this issue. Others will try to tear your marriage apart before it even starts."

Greg added, "It's not only white but black too. Brothers will rag her about not finding a black man. Sisters won't give her as much of a hard time. All Harold and I are saying is just be careful and know where you stand on this issue."

Doug thought about the advice given to him by Harold and Greg. He knew that he and Lisa had to have a difficult talk.

Chapter 10

Lisa and Doug carpooled to work on a rainy Wednesday morning. Lisa missed her private time in the car listening to her thoughts but at the same time enjoyed their time together and getting rest on the way. She played R & B music and he started singing one of the tunes on the radio. She couldn't help but to laugh as he was a little off key.

Doug glanced over and said, "I made an appointment for us to go to Aradia's photography for our engagement announcement photo. Aradia was a good friend of my dad's."

"I hadn't thought that far Doug. I guess we should make a newspaper announcement. I don't want your phone to start ringing again." She snickered at the thought of their first informal date when Doug tried desperately to call women who were too busy for him.

Doug smiled and winked at Lisa. "You can take the jinx off my phone now."

"No way. I'm not taking any chances. I'm pregnant too. I may buy my own pistol to make you go through with it. I never expected to get pregnant before I turned thirty. I wasn't having any children this fast."

"Too late Lisa. We were meant to be together all three of us."

"Lisa smiled and sighed. "Yes, I know."

Lisa arrived at work and settled in her office. After making a few phone calls, she wanted to see if Mona was available for lunch.

Mona shut the door. "I'm so excited that you and Doug are expecting." Mona's face was beaming with pride.

"Mona, I'm still in shock. Everything has happened so fast. I still remember walking in your office on my first day at Grant & Company."

"Sometimes things must happen quickly in order for them to happen at all. This baby was destined to be here by any means necessary. The baby required the two of you to create it."

Lisa smiled at Mona. Mona strongly believed in destiny and fate. "Thank you, Mona. We're planning the wedding for February. My mother and my sister are helping with it. They don't want me to stress because of the pregnancy. Doug and I will give you all the details as they evolve."

"If there's anything I can do to help let me know."

"I will."

"Thank you Lisa. I look forward to all of your good news."

***

Doug was in his office working on a pre-trial motion. He looked up when he noticed Mark Steward at his door. Mark entered and sat in front of Doug with a grim look on his face.

"George Stevens requested that another attorney handle his case."

Doug stared at Mark. He was confused by his statement. He got along very well with his clients and couldn't imagine why George would make a request for another attorney. "Did he say why?"

"He's taking issue with your personal life."

"What? What's my personal life have to do with anything?" Doug sat back in his chair, confused about what this was all about.

"Yes, I did, Doug, but he's taking issue with you being engaged to Lisa. He's one of those racist bigots that old money makes," Mark said.

"This is because of my relationship with Lisa? That's bull shit, Mark, and you know it!"

"It is, but, look, Doug, your personal life is not the business of this firm. Whitman Stacks is an equal opportunity employer. That includes spouses or soon to be spouses of employees. But that doesn't mean we're not going to face some fallout because of your choices. I mean, we anticipate new clients because of them too." Mark leaned forward in his chair. "I just wanted to let you know this personally so you didn't hear it as gossip."

Doug took in his coworker's expression, the mix of bored indifference and casual judgment. Maybe George wasn't the only one who wasn't okay with Doug's choices, but Mark had to play nice since they worked together. He grit his teeth as he responded politely. "I appreciate your professionalism in this matter."

Mark rose, hesitating before the closed door. "Off the record, Doug, and for your personal knowledge, there are partners that take issue with your personal life. I convinced them that times are changing and we must change with the times but…" he shrugged.

Doug didn't get the impression that Mark was all for Doug's relationship either. Mark plastered on his office smile and opened the door, "We'll see you at the Dupree Country Club next week?" He didn't wait for Doug to answer the rhetorical question, closing the door behind him on his way out of Doug's office.

Doug inhaled and sighed. He and Lisa would have to have that discussion sooner rather than later.

***

Doug arrived home later that evening, thinking about the past few days. He knew that he was fully committed to Lisa and was unsure of how to approach the subject of being a biracial couple with her. Lisa was in the kitchen preparing chicken and rice. He snuck up behind her, grabbed her hips and landed a peck on the nape of her neck.

Lisa felt the scratchy sensation of his beard against the softness of her skin. She looked down at his pale hands across her firm abdomen. She stopped what she was doing to turn around and get a full view of her man. Heated kisses moved down her cheek to the front of collarbone. She moaned with delight, leaned back against the countertop. "Ooh, I like those. How was your day?"

"Better, seeing you here at home." Doug relaxed with Lisa in his arms.

"Dinner is ready. Do you want to eat now?" She asked.

His face turned serious. "Let's go talk in the living room. We'll eat later."

With Lisa still in his arms, he guided her into the living room and motioned for her to have a seat.

She sat on the edge of the couch watching Doug as he paced across the floor.

"What's wrong? You have something heavy on your mind."

Doug stopped pacing to answer. "It's something that's never come up between us." Doug took a breath and knelt in front of Lisa to take her hands. "Have you thought about the racial issues that could come up with us getting married?"

Lisa drew a deep breath and let out a long sigh. She was relieved that he brought up the subject first. "Doug, I have. I haven't been able to come up with a way to bring it up to you. Everything happened so fast. What with our relationship and the quick engagement. Now the baby has put a different light on everything."

"Lisa, I don't know what to say. I've never had to deal with this as an issue."

"It's always been an issue for me. When you're in a minority, these issues are front and center. The thought never crossed my mind that I could be in an interracial marriage. My family and your family have, for the most part, been very supportive. It's the people outside of our families that don't know us that are going to have issues."

Doug sat beside Lisa and pulled her close. "Until I met you, I never thought of being in an interracial marriage. You and I were dealing with so many other issues that the fact that we were from different cultural backgrounds, for me, was a plus. I've never met anyone else like you."

Lisa grasped his hand tightly. The warmness of his flesh and the kindness of his words were bringing her closer to a man who was becoming a natural part of her soul. She gave him an encouraging response. "I know this is new for you. I'm here to support you on it."

"If we agree to face it together, there'll be nothing that we can't overcome."

Lisa got up and pulled Doug's hand until he stood with her and followed where she led.

"Where are we going, Lisa?"

"I'm not hungry yet." Lisa raced up the stairs with Doug trailing her lead.

Chapter 11

Terri and Lisa planned a shopping trip to set up her gift registry at a department store.

Terri picked up a designer cup and held it out for Lisa's approval or dislike. "I still can't believe you're pregnant. You wouldn't talk about your feelings for Doug at all and now you're getting married and having his baby."

"Everything has happened so fast. I can't believe it either. We're supposed to go visit his brother, Todd, tomorrow to talk about everything with his side of the family."

"What does Todd think of your marriage?"

"I don't know. I can't tell if Doug's brother is going to be like Mona who is all flowers and kittens about everything, or if he's going to be a jerk about the whole thing. Doug hasn't really said a whole lot about his brother."

"How is Doug handling the pressure?"

"We started talking about them but there will be more discussions."

Terri nodded and replaced the cup on the table and turned back to Lisa. Terri looked off to the distance and a frown creased on her forehead. "Why is that man staring at you?"

Lisa turned to see a well-dressed, short, African American male with glasses and nice dimples. It took her a minute, but she recognized Trent easily enough when he walked closer and she met him with a warm hug. "Well if it isn't Trent Davenport. How are you?"

Trent wrapped her in his arms. "Lisa Dunbar, you're looking as lovely as ever."

She laughed at his usual flirtation, pushing away from his embrace when Terri walked over. She pulled her sister close for introductions. "This is my sister Terri; Terri, this is my friend, Trent Davenport."

Trent nodded politely to Terri but turned his gaze back to Lisa without really noticing her sister. It had been so long since he'd seen her, and his feelings for her had never really changed. He smiled, hoping now was the time to get her back. "What brings you to the mall?"

"Bridal registry! I'm getting married in February!"

Trent was startled by her revelation. "Congratulations, who's the lucky man?"

"I actually introduced you to him—Doug Bader?"

"That white, I mean," Trent stumbled over his words, looking from the sister to Lisa and back again, hoping it was a joke, and knowing it wasn't. "Well…I wish happiness for the both of you, Lisa."

"Thank you, Trent."

"I'm here to get my mom a birthday present so I will leave you lovely ladies to continue shopping." Trent warmly smiled at Lisa and nodded to Terri as he walked away.

"What was that about?" Terri asked. "If you hadn't told him that you were engaged I'm sure that he would have asked you out."

While laughing at her sister's comment she said, "He's not my type. I was thinking about introducing him to Maya."

Chapter 12

Lisa and Doug rose early on Saturday morning with a full day of activities scheduled.

Lisa was spoiled by the fact that Doug was always up first to make coffee. She was never one to make a big deal about breakfast but now she had to be concerned for her and the baby. Doug scurried around in his morning hyper mode when she walked into the kitchen. He stopped what he was doing long enough to give Lisa a hug and a morning kiss before moving back to the egg whites frying in the nonstick pan, no butter or salt.

"Decaf for you and 4 ounces only."

As Lisa sat herself at the table, Doug zipped a small teacup in front of her and kissed her on the forehead. She inhaled the brisk smell of the beans and sighed it back out. "Doug, what does your brother think about our engagement?"

Doug paused at the stove and turned to look at her with the spatula half raised. "He was a little surprised but happy for me. I'm glad we're going to dinner at his house today. I know him and his wife are anxious to meet the woman who took Atlanta's Most Eligible Bachelor off the market."

He turned up Lisa's favorite R & B station and started singing along. He butchered a few of the words which made Lisa laugh. He changed to a top forty station and started singing a song that he was familiar with. He extended his hand silently requesting that she dance with him.

Grasping her hips and pulling her tightly next to him he started swaying her from side to side. He rubbed his scratchy cheek next to hers taking in a deep breath closing his eyes and serenading her.

Lisa's heart was pounding fast and breakfast was the last thing on her mind as Doug had her wrapped in his arms. She squeezed his arms tightly and looked up into his eyes. Whatever may have been on her mind was now gone as she pulled him in tightly for a passionate kiss.

Gently moving Lisa away Doug brought himself back into focus and gazed into Lisa's eyes. "Breakfast first, and then rest."

"I'm not hungry yet." She lightly kissed his lips. He laughed and motioned for her to go back to the table. She pretended to pout as he made a plate for her.

"I'm still not hungry yet." She said as she stood up to leave the kitchen. "I'm going upstairs. Joining me?"

"You bet I am."

***

Relaxing in the comfort of the soft bed, Doug reached for Lisa and nestled his face under her ear. He whispered, "Just think, we'll be taking our baby to the library for story time next year."

"And soccer practice." She stroked her had down his arm. "What do you think we're having?"

"A boy first then another boy, then two girls then another boy. Oh, then another girl." Doug grinned at Lisa waiting for her response.

Her mouth dropped open. "Doug, that's six kids! I'm not having that many kids."

"I only mentioned six? I meant seven. I want one for every room in the house." Doug was in full teasing mode. He wanted to see how much of a reaction he could get.

Lisa sat straight up. "Doug, have you lost your mind? I'm not having seven kids! Two, three at the most. The other four will have to be with your next wife."

Doug sat up and hugged her placing a kiss on her cheek. Lisa gave him a light elbow nudge which made him laugh. "Well Doug, seven kids is seven college tuition's, seven private schools, seven kids to dress in the morning, seven different kids' activities, seven..."

Lisa was good at this. Doug hadn't thought of all of the responsibilities with that many kids. He gave up his teasing. "Stop, I get it. I get it... But you did agree to three." Doug chuckled at the look in Lisa's eyes.

Lisa responded, "Two."

"Three...or I go back to seven."

She laughed, enjoying the play between them, the relaxation compared to the stress of all the changes in their lives lately.

***

Doug and Lisa arrived at the library. Doug took his place to read for the children.

Lisa sat at a table close to him and listened to his story. After the reading was over, Doug introduced Lisa to some of the library staff. She spoke with some of the mothers while Doug moved aside to hug one of the children pulling his pant leg.

"I'm Amy. My daughter is Patricia. She's the two year old with Doug. She just love's his readings. Did I hear that the two of you are getting married?"

"Yes, in February."

"That's wonderful." Amy exclaimed. "He's such a neat guy. I wish you both much happiness."

Lisa smiled, "Thank you, Amy."

Doug returned to wrap his arms around Lisa's waist giving her a playful kiss on the cheek.

"See, neat," Amy laughed.

Chapter 13

Lisa and Doug stopped back at his house to change cars since hers had all of the equipment in it. He argued over her driving, but she insisted since she wasn't that far along in the pregnancy and she'd have an emergency stopping brake installed on the passenger side for his comfort after the game. Doug grit his teeth, knowing she was just joking, but uncomfortable all the same. Still, he couldn't take all of her freedoms, so he gave in eventually.

They arrived in time to set up for the soccer game. Doug grabbed the balls out of the trunk and waved her away.

"Doug, it's a sack of balls and I'm not that far along. I can manage this on my own. Why don't you go sit with the parents?"

"Lisa, lots of things can happen in the first trimester of a pregnancy. If you don't want me to help, then get your teenagers to do it."

"I'm not helpless Doug!" she shouted at him. Frustrated, she grabbed a few of the lighter items and started towards the field and Doug quickly followed.

The teenage girls began to arrive and noticed their coach with her fiancé. Lisa glanced at Doug silently telling him that he was no longer needed. He got the message and walked towards the bleachers. On his way there, he was intercepted by a father from the other team.

"I'm Jeff. My daughter is Greta. I saw you set up the cones for Coach Lisa. Are you the new assistant coach for that team?"

Doug declined to extend his hand. He wasn't in the mood to socialize and wasn't sure of Jeff's motives. "Nice to meet you. I'm not a coach. I'm Lisa's fiancé. She isn't allowed to lift anything over ten pounds. I'll be assisting her until well after our baby comes."

Jeff folded his arms and shifted his stance to a solid square posture. He rubbed his beard while he thought of a response.

"Congratulations to you and Lisa. I assumed when you were setting up the cones that you were a coach." Jeff returned to his group of soccer parents and proceeded to spread the gossip.

Doug took a seat on the bleachers. All of the parents of Lisa's soccer team were aware of her engagement to Doug. Some parents were friendlier than others which had no effect on Doug. He was here to ensure that Lisa didn't overdo it.

The game moved to half time and Doug left to go to the concession stand. He was standing in line to get a drink. Someone tapped Doug on the shoulder from behind. Doug turned around and met Jeff's stare.

"I didn't get your name earlier."

"I'm Doug."

"Forgive my nosiness, but how in the world did you meet Lisa?"

Doug shifted and crossed his arms, starting to get annoyed at Jeff's tone, not sure if the man was just that bold or genuinely curious. "It's a long story."

"That must have been tough to decide to get married and deal with all the racial stuff."

Doug assessed Jeff's question. Jeff looked harmless but was not someone that he wanted to have a conversation about his personal life with Lisa. Doug gave a noncommittal answer hoping that this man would go back to his team. "Lisa and I handle all challenges as they come. There is nothing more to discuss about that."

That was better than telling the guy straight up to stay out of his business, but Doug hoped his reaction didn't hurt Lisa or her team.

Chapter 14

Doug and Lisa arrived at Todd's house around 6:00pm. His brother answered the door and Doug warmly greeted him with a hug, moving aside to introduce everyone. "Todd, this is my fiancée, Lisa. Lisa, my brother, Todd."

Todd fought not to let his jaw drop when he got a good look at Lisa. She wasn't what he expected and Doug never mentioned that she was black. He awkwardly extended his hand to her, unsure what exactly he should do. "Nice to meet you, Lisa."

"You too, Todd."

After their greetings, Todd invited them in and said his children were staying with friends.

Alice walked out of the kitchen to see Doug and meet his fiancée. She smiled warmly at Lisa and offered to take her on a tour of their home.

They ended up in the kitchen after Alice showed Lisa around the upstairs and the family room downstairs. The house was very rustic with hardwood floors and several antiques.

"Please, take a seat. I've just got to get the venison out of the oven. Doug always says he loves my venison when I make it so I thought it would be a nice treat. It's my favorite recipe too."

Lisa sat down at the table and tried to smile politely, not sure that she wanted a taste of Bambi. Her stomach was rebelling because of the baby and not from the idea of eating deer.

Alice grabbed a pitcher of sweet tea from the fridge and poured Lisa a glass. "It's nice to finally meet you…"

"It's nice to finally meet you. Doug is really excited about getting married."

"I'm excited too."

Alice sat directly across from her. Nothing came to mind to say to Lisa. "I'm so excited to meet you but I'm not sure what to say!" Alice laughed and it was a comfortable, friendly sound meant to put Lisa at ease.

Lisa suggested, "We could talk about the weather, music, stars, what you've read in a magazine, your kids, your family… There's a lot to talk about."

"Okay then! I'll tell you a little about me. My parents came from a working class background. They sacrificed to put me through private school. That is where I met Doug and Todd. I was a freshman, Todd was a sophomore and Doug was a senior. Todd and I were really good friends. We always stayed in touch. I worked part-time during the summer for Bader Construction during high school and that's where I became friends with Todd.

Alice continued, "After I graduated high school, I was tired of school and the arguments with my parents. One day, Todd called me to work for his company full time. I worked there for a year and somehow Todd and I became more than friends. We started with dinner occasionally. It moved from occasionally to very often. Since the death of Todd's parents, he seemed to bury himself in his work. At the same time, he seemed to need me more. If he wasn't working, he was with me. Two years later we got married and have been happy ever since."

Lisa was amazed, "Wow, didn't the both of you marry young?"

Alice smiled. "I was twenty-one and he was twenty-two. Neither one of us went to college. Todd's father wanted him to go but Todd decided to run the business. Doug was always the bright one though. After his parents died, he really buried himself in his college studies. I mean, I had Todd, but Doug was pretty much alone. Everyone was dealing their grief separately. Has Doug told you about that already?"

"No ma'am, he hasn't mentioned it. I just know they passed away."

"Oh, I just assumed...well," Alice paused. "You really should know though, just, please don't repeat it unless he asks you." She took a sip of her tea and Lisa followed suit. "Doug's parents and his girlfriend were driving to his dorm to pick him up for spring break. I just know they got into a car accident and all three of them were killed. They were all gone in a moment, even before they got to the hospital. Neither Doug nor Todd had a chance to say goodbye"

"We figured Doug would never settle down after losing Tiffany, but, then he called about you and, well, it's just terrific, Lisa. I'm so happy for you both."

Lisa tried to smile back at the other women in light of the tragic story. But clearly Alice was determined to keep the evening friendly despite the sadness, so Lisa did her best to respond accordingly. "Thank you. That means a lot to me. Did Doug tell you how we met?"

"No, he hasn't."

Chapter 15

After the women left to tour the home, Todd and Doug retired to the deck so that they could have a private talk.

Doug hadn't brought a woman to meet his brother since the car accident that took the life of their parents.

"Doug, what are you trying to do, throw your career out the window?" Todd's face was grim. His eyebrows crinkled and his tone of voice moved to a higher pitch, which was normal for Todd when he got upset.

Doug crossed his arms and met his brother's stare. "What are you talking about? Throw away my career? Why would I do that?"

"She's black Doug. You're a southern lawyer. You couldn't find a southern white woman, one that won't get pregnant on purpose."

"That's not the way it happened. I chose not to use precaution the night we got engaged. Lay off of Lisa. It was my responsibility. This pregnancy has just moved the wedding up."

Todd squared his shoulders and faced Doug directly. "This romance has happened really fast. She could be after your money."

"She doesn't know what I have. Give it up Todd."

"How many clients do you think you're going to keep when they see you've got a black wife and black kids? You'll have to move up north if you ever want to make any money practicing law."

"I'm not moving and business is fine. Stay out of it. Lisa is perfect for me."

"No she's not. You don't know that coon"

Doug grabbed his brother by the shirt collar pressing his nose against his. "Don't you ever say that to my face again."

"Let go of me. Better you hear me tell it to you than someone else."

"It's better you keep that to yourself. Alice doesn't know about the 3-year old you've got."

Todd turned an ashen white. "How did you know about that?"

"I've got friends" Doug replied smugly.

***

Alice summoned the men to come eat. The meal was very silent. Doug didn't sip his vodka tonic and held Lisa's hand tightly under the table.

Todd glanced over at Lisa and Doug with a concerned expression. The brothers were angry with each other. Lisa and Alice's conversation was stilted.

"Lisa, what is your line of work?"

"I work for Doug's Aunt Mona as a CPA."

Todd perked up and took special notice of Lisa's statement. He threw his napkin on the table and crossed his leg one over the other.

"How long have you worked for my Aunt Mona?" Todd asked.

"I started working for her about two months ago."

"When did you meet my brother?" Todd's eyes narrowed and his face now held a grim expression.

Lisa laughed. "Actually, I met him the evening of my first day at work. I was ordering take out…"

Doug finished for her, "…and she refused to give me her name." Doug looked at his brother and returned the tense expression.

Lisa laughed, trying to lighten the mood of the brothers. "Doug bought dinner for me anyway. I just walked out the door."

Alice asked, "So you must have met again at another time?"

Doug answered dryly, "We did."

Doug was in no mood to repeat the story and Todd was in no mood to hear it. Alice got up to leave the table to answer the phone.

"Lisa, we have another appointment this evening. I'm sorry to cut this visit short." Lisa took Doug's cue and rose to leave with him. Dinner was tense enough and she was ready to go. Todd walked Doug and Lisa to the door.

"I'll tell Alice that you've left. Let me show you the way out."

Todd and Doug gave each other a final stare before parting at the door. Doug held Lisa's hand firmly as they walked to the driveway.

Doug was silent in the car on the way home, quietly seething while Lisa sat next to him wondering what she could do to fix whatever had happened between him and his brother.

Once they arrived home, Doug brushed his lips softly against her cheek. "I'm going to the study for a while."

"Okay."

He walked down the hall, grateful Lisa didn't try to pry.

Doug hadn't anticipated having issues with his brother. He'd fully expected Todd to be happy for him. He closed the door and fixed a Vodka tonic to relax his nerves and mull over the talk with his brother.

***

Lisa made herself busy for the next hour. She also reflected on the brief visit at his brother's home. Doug didn't have a lot of family and was closest to his Aunt Mona. Lisa could feel Todd's iciness and, bless her heart, Alice displayed her southern manners well and didn't know what to make of the situation until after talking with Lisa. Maybe Todd would come around.

As Lisa was napping in the sunroom, Doug quietly walked in. He knelt beside her, taking her hand into his, feeling the warm energy flow through her veins. He couldn't resist her. She was his ideal woman.

Doug's touch woke her. She blinked and stared into his eyes, the deep hurt that lurked within. She hoped he was willing to share. "Are you okay, Doug?"

Doug answered in a deep slow voice exhaling his frustration in an apologetic manner. "I had a lot on my mind. Todd and I were arguing. I really didn't like what he said. That's why I wanted to leave in the middle of dinner."

Lisa's eyes didn't wander as she softly stroked his soft sandy blonde hair. "I knew something was wrong. I didn't want to press you for information. I felt that you would tell me about it if you wanted me to know."

Doug released some stress feeling Lisa's gentle touch. "I don't want to discuss our argument. I didn't want you to believe that I was angry with you. My brother is a moron."

Doug stood up still frustrated with the argument he had with his brother. He started pacing the floor "I just can't believe my brother would be such an asshole about this."

"What, Doug?"

"He was fixated on the fact that you were black. He's the first one in my family that's been a dick about it, and he's my brother."

"We all got asshole family members."

"This is my brother. We've only got each other with my parents gone. He should be happy for me."

"He'll come around. I know you didn't tell him that I was black. I saw the look on his face when I got to the door. It was priceless." Lisa snickered.

"How can you sit there and laugh about?"

"Why didn't you tell him that I was black?"

"What!" Doug paused in place and crinkled his eyebrows. He couldn't believe her question.

"Why didn't you tell him I was black?" Lisa stood up and faced him squarely.

"I don't know. It wasn't important. It still isn't. I figured he'd be happy for me what with—never mind."

"Never mind what. You wanted to see his reaction. Admit it. I've done the same thing. Depending on the situation, I only say I have a fiancé but this is family and they need more information."

Doug slightly grinned after thinking over her observation. "Okay, I still didn't expect his reaction."

Lisa locked her arms behind his neck and pulled him close. Doug nestled his face under Lisa's chin. "Dealing with difficult family members are part of the obstacles we will face. I love you, Doug. There's no changing that."

Chapter 16

It was the morning of Thanksgiving. Lisa's parents were hosting the holiday party. Doug was a little nervous because his holiday events had always been small but now he was going to be reintroduced to Lisa's many family members.

Usually, he spent time with Mona and they travelled together to visit her children during the fall. This year was different. Now he was engaged and was expecting children of his own.

Lisa rose early to make a sweet potato casserole. She grabbed her left-handed mixer that Doug had purchased for her and the whizzing sound blared throughout the house. She'd almost completed her dish when she heard Doug coming into the kitchen.

Lisa asked, "Are you ready to meet my family?"

"I think so."

"Too bad Mona couldn't come. Which one of her children is she staying with?"

"Amy. Amy and Susie live in Raleigh, and Bruce lives in Orlando. Bruce and Mona are flying to Raleigh for the holiday."

"Have you told your cousins about me?" Lisa asked.

"I rarely talk to them but, knowing Aunt Mona, she's told everyone."

Lisa laughed. She finished preparing her the casserole and they left for the family holiday dinner.

Lisa and Doug arrived and started mingling with her family. Ann and Dave had a full house of relatives. The men were in the den and the women were in the kitchen.

Dave came over to Doug to shake his hand and led him to the living room for some food. There was a corner table that contained a huge spread of appetizers which included deviled eggs, assorted fruits and cheeses, raw vegetable tray, and spinach dip in a pumpernickel bowl. There was absolutely too much for Doug to choose from. He took some of the dip but refrained from the eggs to save room for dinner.

Doug sat on the couch and was taking bites of an appetizer when he overheard a conversation going on behind him. He recognized Ricky's voice, having memorized it at Terri's wedding. He didn't recognize the voice of the other man.

"I can't believe Terri's sister is marrying that white guy." Ricky said with a tone of disgust.

"I can't believe it either. This engagement was a shock to the family." The other man said in a low deep voice.

"Terri says she's pregnant too." Ricky groused.

Doug leaned forward to pretend he was eavesdropping when Terri interrupted the conversation and offered the men something to drink. They continued after she left.

"I get enough of white men at work. I don't want to see them on my free time. She couldn't find a brother that was good enough for her?"

A man's voice responded. "I met Jaylon. That brother is an attorney, had the house and everything. Lisa and him dated for two years then broke it off. Everyone thought that they were getting married. This thing with Doug has really surprised the family. This entire thing has happened in less than three months."

Ricky lowered his tone of voice which made it difficult for Doug to hear the rest of the conversation, not that Doug had long to listen when Dave returned and started talking about the upcoming football game.

Chapter 17

Stacy yelled out to Lisa first. "Girl where did you find that good looking white man?"

All the women laughed.

"I met him at a restaurant."

Stacy slung her braids back behind her ear. "He got a brother?"

"His brother is married." Lisa answered.

"Don't get him wet, he'll smell like dog hair." The voice that came out of nowhere was Lisa's Aunt Lucille.

"Leave my baby girl alone and let her live a little life." Ann said as she shooed the cousins out of the kitchen.

The cousins headed for the door and moved their conversation to the family room leaving the Aunts to finish reminiscing and cooking the meal. The cousins settled in and got comfortable on the couch.

Stacy's curiosity couldn't be contained. "How are you handling the black white thing?"

"Not you too. Why are you grilling me on it?"

"I just want to know. Is it true that all white guys are short?"

Lisa laughed. "Not Doug. Maybe he's not white."

All the cousins laughed.

"Are you going to teach Doug the Electric Slide? He may get it. I saw him dancing with you at my wedding. He's got a little rhythm for a white guy." The cousins snickered at Terri's comment.

"Doug's moves are just fine. You are as bad as our aunties. I may have to go upstairs and sit with them. You guys are mean." Lisa throws a pillow at her sister.

Maya asked, "Can he sing? Are you bringing him to church?"

Lisa responded. "I don't know yet. We haven't discussed church, and no, singing is not his strongest talent." The girls howled.

"So what do you want? Boy or Girl" Terri asked.

"It doesn't matter as long as it's only one kid." Lisa said with delighted voice. "Doug wants a house full of kids and three is my limit."

Stacy said, "I heard that his house is huge. Are you going to work after the baby is born?"

"I plan to work, coach soccer and do everything I do now." Lisa stood up and rubbed her firm abdomen. "See, I'm in great shape."

"Babies are a lot of work." Stacy said. "I'm not planning on kids for a long time."

Maya crinkled her nose and spoke up, "Lisa, I don't know if I could get a white boyfriend. Dealing with the racism would bother me."

Lisa answered. "Everything bothers you Maya. We can't get you to go out with anyone black, white or otherwise. You are extremely picky."

Maya responded, "I can't help it. I've watched the three of you fall in love and get heartbroken. I want no part of that."

Stacy said, "You're not going to find your true love on the first date. Maya, you don't get to the second date. How are you going to know anything about a man if you don't see him more than one time?"

Maya turned up her nose, "That's okay. I'm not getting treated like dirt."

"I thought you wanted children?" Terri said.

"I do. When I turn thirty, I'll adopt. I turn twenty nine in March so I have a year to think about it."

Ann called for the women to return to the kitchen to help finish the Thanksgiving preparations and they trudged back into the lion's den of turkey and casseroles.

***

Once the basement was free, the men moved downstairs while the women were completing the dinner. Doug was on his third Vodka tonic because he and Lisa had agreed that she would be the designated driver. The way the evening was going for Doug, a few more Vodka tonics would be in order to get through it, but he couldn't lose it in front of his soon to be new relatives.

Ricky cornered Doug near the fireplace. The two men glared at each other with enough distance to hold their space. Doug wasn't going to back down but had no intention of starting an altercation.

"So what made you decide to marry a sistah?" Ricky's moustache twitched and the ice in his glass clicked as he swallowed the last of his cocktail.

Doug was on empty and he'd left his glass behind on the coffee table. Ricky's question struck a nerve. He sensed that this conversation was not friendly and would turn into an argument if he didn't act diplomatically. Doug remembered his brief encounter with Ricky at the wedding rehearsal. Other times had been cordial and distant. This didn't feel like one of those time. "I'm in love with Lisa. I didn't want to wait any longer."

"I know your family doesn't approve of this." Ricky watched Doug with suspicion.

Doug carefully crafted his answer. "My family is the same as Lisa's family. Some members approve and some don't. We're not taking a vote from our relatives to see if we should get married."

"How many black women have you dated?"

Doug continued his glare at Ricky but kept control of his emotions. His shoulders were tense and his breathing hastened. He took deep breaths to calm down. Remembering his courtroom training, he momentarily composed himself as if he were at a hearing for a guilty client. Never show your hand and never let them see you sweat. "Just Lisa."

"You're a rich white guy that could have any woman you wanted. Why do you want a black woman?"

Doug felt his fingers tighten at his sides. It would be so easy to shut Ricky up, but he knew that it wasn't the right way to deal with the situation.

Luckily, Dave interceded, again, unknowingly.

"Doug, Ricky can I get either of you something to drink?"

Doug's face was a light shade of red and Ricky was angry as well.

"Vodka on the rocks with a twist," Doug answered.

"Gin and juice. A black man's drink."

The two continued to glare at each other.

"Doug, why don't you come help me grab the drinks? Ricky, I think Ray wants to see you."

"Whatever." Ricky turned away and Doug couldn't help the exhale, relieved to be away from the entire situation that was beginning to take a turn for the worse.

"Ricky is a pain in the ass but a lot of black men feel the same way he does. Doug, this will not be an easy marriage for you and Lisa. There will be a lot of outside pressure from blacks as well as whites."

Doug nodded in agreement but didn't know what to say. "I should check on Lisa."

"Lisa's fine. Let me get your drink. Dinner should be ready soon."

Chapter 18

Doug and Lisa were side by side looking at the variety of food including: ham, turkey, meatloaf, chicken, chitterlings, hog maws, greens, macaroni and cheese, okra, squash, black-eyed peas, green bean casserole, purple cabbage, mashed potatoes, dressing, and cornbread. Deciding what to eat was nearly impossible after having appetizers before the meal.

Dave said the blessing as all of the Dunbar family stood in a circle and held hands with their heads bowed thinking about what they were thankful for. Lisa's lips parted with a small smile as her eyes darted over to Doug who had her hand firmly clasped in his.

Doug's eyes were closed as his mind wandered thinking about the new life that was coming and his impending marriage. His life had changed so drastically. Doug spent holidays with Greg's family on occasion so Thanksgiving with Lisa's family seemed very similar.

After the blessing was said, some family members made their way to the table to claim their place while others started through the kitchen to prepare their plates.

As Lisa prepared her plate, she glanced over at Doug's plate. Much to her surprise, Doug added a few chitterlings and hog maws to his plate. After they sat down she watched as Doug started eating. Her forehead crinkled and she tugged Doug's sleeve as he was about to stick his fork into his plate. "Do you know what you're eating?"

Doug glanced back at her with an affirmative smile. "Yes, I believe these are chit-lings "

By this time a few other family members paused to look at Doug. Some had looks of amazement on their faces, not having figured him to actually know what they were.

"You're going to eat that?" Lisa asked.

Doug laughed and said "Yup. Would you pass the hot sauce and cha cha?"

Lisa laughed as she grabbed the hot sauce and passed it to him. Doug picked up the bottle and shook the contents until the chitterlings were almost completely covered. He took his spoon and dropped a big dollop of cha cha on top.

Lisa continued to stare at Doug. "Do you know what those are? "She asked as she almost laughed through her question.

"They are pig intestines and pig stomach. I've had them at Greg's mom's house. She makes other strange stuff too. My brother and I have gone to the

Road Kill festival just for kicks to see what people actually do with it."

"Oh, that's gross," Lisa sighed in disgust.

Doug smiled and winked at her. "I'll take you there for our anniversary. Do you want some of my chit-lings? They're pretty good."

Aunt Lucille's head popped up from the other end of the table. She smiled and winked at Doug. "Thank you, I'll let you get the first piece of my pecan pie."

"No ma'am. I don't mean to offend you but I'm allergic to pecans."

Lucille's jaw dropped with slight disappointment. "I do have cream cheese cake with caramel frosting."

"I'm in." Doug said with a grin. Lisa rolled her eyes, amused with Doug's interaction with her aunt. Doug noticed Lisa's plate was absent of chitterlings and he made her another offer.

"Have some." He stuck his fork into his plate and picked up a piece that had a lot of cha cha on top. He placed his hand under it so it wouldn't fall off.

"I don't eat those."

"Try some for me. I promise. It's really good this way."

With her family watching to see what she would do, she opened her mouth and allowed Doug to place the morsel into her mouth. She chewed the piece and her face was expressionless. She was still chewing slowly as she was deciding whether or not she liked it. "It's ok Doug but no more. You enjoy them."

"So are you going to make these for Christmas?" Doug said as he reached his arm across her shoulder to give her a light hug.

Lisa cut her eyes at Doug. She drew her lips closer to his and whispered sweetly, "Not on your life."

Doug released her and laughed.

"White people eating chit-lins. Now I've seen it all." Aunt Olivia's strong voice broke the silence of the room after Doug's display, the humor in her eyes making Lisa smile. "I was surprised that you knew what they were and had no problem eating them."

"I won't get into the wild game discussion at the table. I want Lisa to enjoy her food."

"Wild game discussion?" Lisa asked.

Doug laughed at Lisa and told her, "Later."

Aunt O leaned back in her chair and just stared while Lisa laughed and kissed Doug's cheek. "Okay. Thank you, I think."

The discussion turned to politics and the upcoming presidential election. The debate between family members got heated about the Republican agenda. Doug and Lisa listened in as her parents discussed the issues with her Uncle Ray. Others were having smaller private chats.

Ray was seated next to Doug and asked him, "Are you a Democrat or Republican?"

"Ray!" Ann shouted. "That's none of your business."

"Independent" Doug answered in a noncommittal voice.

"So you don't take sides or you just don't want to join a party?"

"I'm an attorney. I can debate both sides of any issue. I choose not to pick a party. It can limit my clientele."

"I bet you're a closet Republican," Ray said with a chuckle. "All white men are, especially in the South."

Doug shrugged it off and didn't engage any further into the conversation and changed the subject. "Are you retired?"

"Hell no," Ray exclaimed. "I own Ray's New and Used Suits. No retiring for me. Maya, that's my daughter," he nodded down the table to the woman at Lisa's side, "She works in my store part-time. I'm hoping she'll take over the shop once I give it up. I've been in business for twenty years."

"I've heard of Ray's. My friend Greg shops there all the time. He's a corporate executive that travels a lot."

Ray leaned back in his chair. "Greg Speaks? I know him. He's at the shop a lot. The next time you see him tell, you him you met me."

"I will."

Ricky was stoic at the table glancing at Doug occasionally. Doug glanced back at him with his icy blue eyes. He wasn't going to let Ricky intimidate him in front of Lisa and her family.

Ricky turned up his nose and said, "I bet you're an Alabama fan, cracker."

Doug fought to keep the smile on his face, trying to curb his sarcastic reply even as it came to his lips. "That's saltine American to you." He put down his fork and took Lisa's hand, figuring that the other members around the table would want information, even if they would have asked in a more polite way. "I went to Emory. So it's Tech or UGA for me."

Ricky's fact lit up and he howled across the table, "Dawg's rule" and he barked out loud with the men at the table joining him.

Doug laughed and the women shook their heads, exasperated.

They had almost escaped a night of football arguments.

Dave asked Doug "The Peach Bowl is coming up. Are you going?"

"My fried Eric gave me tickets. If you want to go, I'll see if he can get more."

Dave smiled, impressed with his future son-in-law's connections.

As the dinner conversation wound down the women went back into the kitchen talking about family gossip. They washed dishes and divvied up the remains of dinner to take to each one's respective households.

The men began moving furniture, putting up chairs and settling into the afternoon TV watching. Although Doug sat comfortably with the men, he began to get concerned that Lisa could be tired from all of the activities. He entered the doorway and gazed at her from across the room hoping that she would notice that he was ready to leave.

She stopped her conversation with Terri when she saw him. "Are you ready to go?"

"Whenever you are."

She winked at Doug. "Let me wrap up some things to take home with us and then we can get going."

"Don't forget to take his chit-lins," Aunt Lucille said in a half smirking laugh. "He may not see any more before next year."

Chapter 19

To take advantage of black Friday shopping, Lisa arrived at Terri's house early. Ann was already there when she arrived so they packed into Ann's van and headed to the bridal store to look at wedding dresses.

After trying on numerous dresses, Lisa settled on a princess gown that was a couple of sizes larger to allow room for her pregnancy. She gazed into the mirror lost into her thoughts as her mother and sister oohed and awed over the dress.

"Wow Lisa, you look gorgeous."

Lisa's smile brightened as she imagined her wedding day to Doug being full of happiness and love for a man that she was taking a leap of faith with.

"Thanks, Terri. I really like this dress."

"I think it's perfect for you." Ann said. "I'm really happy for the both of you."

"Thanks, mom." Lisa hugged both her sister and her mother. A few tears rolled down her face.

"Now what are those?" Ann asked half-jokingly, hugging her daughter while Lisa cried.

"My daughter never cries."

Lisa laughed as she wiped her tears away. "I don't know where they came from and don't tell anyone that you saw them."

"Lisa's in love." Terri said, drying a few tears of her own.

"Let's get out of here before I ruin the dress."

Later in the afternoon, Lisa and Terri were discussing wedding plans in the Terri's kitchen. It was decided that the wedding was going to be at Dupree Country Club where Doug had a few connections.

A last minute cancellation put the wedding in the first weekend in February, perfect since Lisa shouldn't be showing too much then.

Ricky and his friend Chris came by around lunch/dinner time. Lisa and Terri greeted the men as they raided the refrigerator and prepared snacks for themselves without offering any to Lisa and Terri.

"Ricky tells me that you're marrying some white guy," Chris said, a harsh tone to his voice.

"He's not just some white guy. His name is Doug Bader." Lisa glared at Chris, preparing for a verbal battle.

Chris pressed further. "So the brothers weren't good enough for you?" He snorted in derision.

Lisa had turned Chris down some time ago. Apparently his ego was still bruised but Lisa wasn't going to put up with his smart tone. "That has nothing to do with why we're getting married." She didn't have to justify her marriage to Doug to anyone. Especially a jerk and a menace like Chris.

"Wedding's kind of fast though. What are you pregnant or something?"

Lisa stood up and Terri jumped to her side. "That is none of your concern. Go home and take care of your own woman. Oh wait, you don't have one, do you?" Lisa put her hands on her hips and met Chris' gaze evenly.

Terri and Ricky howled with laughter.

"Look, all of my women have been sistahs. What's your excuse?"

"I like men, first off, so I wouldn't be dating any sistahs anyways. And Doug's marrying me. What's your excuse for getting them pregnant and leaving them?" Lisa crossed her arms and felt Terri's hand on her arm. She flicked her arm to make Terri release her. "You don't want to go there with me." She'd taken on many battles in her life and this one she could handle without her sister's interference.

"It's hard for a brother in a white man's world. If you think white people are going to accept you with him, they won't."

Lisa kept her composure but made sure he understood her loud and persistent tone. "I don't give a care what anybody thinks. This relationship is between Doug and me. You can step your wanna be working self right out of my business."

"Why are you harassing my sister, Chris? Black men pick up white women all the time. You both have friends and relatives that do it and you never say a word to them."

Ricky answered his wife, "That's different."

Terri glared at him. "How so?" She crossed her arms as she stared at him. "I would be careful if I were you as to how you answer that question."

Chris stuck out his chest. "It is different. Sistahs are supposed to support the brothers."

"How about the brothers are supposed to support the sistahs. That looks like nonsupport to me."

Ricky dove right into the argument, "So you are saying that black women should give up and find men that aren't black like you did." Ricky's interference had Lisa smoldering.

"Black women should find the best available mate that will support them regardless of race. If Doug were black, we wouldn't be having this conversation."

"Damn straight," Chris said. "He isn't black. You're just another black woman birthing white men's children."

Lisa grabbed her coat and purse. She marched over to the kitchen door brushing past Chris. Terri followed Lisa and tried to stop her.

"Terri, I'm out of here. I will no longer take these insults." Out the door and to her car she went with Terri following her. She yelled out to Lisa as she had her hand on the door handle. Chris and Ricky remained in the house.

"You shouldn't let that fool get to you."

"The fool is in your house and you didn't ask him to leave. One of us had to go. I'll be back over when he is not here." Lisa got in her car and drove off.

***

Doug was at home when Lisa came marching in the door. He heard her footsteps while he was reviewing a case, and lifted his head to meet her gaze when she found him in the study. She looked angry, stressed maybe while she stood in the doorway. Doug paused, peered over his glasses and looked directly into her dark brown eyes.

"I hate Chris and Ricky." She said in a very angry tone. "I don't know why she married him."

"You mean your brother-in-law, the one with the good values?" Doug asked sarcastically.

"Are you going to start an argument with me?"

"No Lisa, I'm not. What did he say to you?" Doug rounded the desk to get closer to Lisa. He didn't like the things that Ricky had said to him but he definitely didn't want Lisa insulted under any circumstances. She was his love and no one was coming between them.

"The why am I marrying a white guy stupidity. It's none of his business. I can marry who I want."

Doug stood there studying Lisa's face. She pouted and crossed her arms still trying to calm down from her incident with Chris. Doug kissed her lightly on the forehead. "What do you want to do about it?"

Doug's kiss spread through her veins lighting a torch in the core of her being. She pulled Doug's hips close to hers, tilted her head back and kissed him, pressing her breasts tightly into his chest. She pulled his shirt out of his pants and ran her hands over his chest.

Doug was hard where their hips pressed together. He slipped his hands beneath her sweatshirt and cupped her breasts through her bra.

Lisa leaned back, threw off her shirt, and put her hands on Doug's shoulders as he reached around her to unclasp her bra and pull it from her body. She stepped out of her sweatpants. He caressed her soft brown skin.

Lisa removed her sweatshirt exposing her swollen breasts. Doug's tongue licked around each one causing Lisa to moan. "Careful, they're tender."

Doug guided Lisa back to the desk and sat in the executive chair. He slowly turned her on his lap, facing away from him. She moaned as he thrust up into her body.

Lisa braced herself against the desk pushing back against Doug so he could invade her thoroughly. Lisa reached her peak and let out a loud sigh with a last push from Doug as he came too with a final moan.

"You should get angry more often."

Lisa turned her head and looked at Doug. Her eyes narrowed at his remark, and she couldn't help slugging him in the chest playfully.

He howled in mock pain and stood up quickly, pulling her with him, his hands wrapped around her wrists so he wouldn't receive any more punishment.

Lisa playfully tried to break free but with him being the strongest of the pair, couldn't manage it.

He released her wrists only so he could turn her and press his reawakening arousal against her backside.

"Let me go Doug." Before she could say it again, he kissed the back of her neck, reached to cup her chin and turn her head to face him, cover her mouth with a strong willful kiss.

She turned in his arms to hold him, succumbing to his advances by relaxing her body and locking her hands into his arms with a tight grip. She gazed into Doug's deep blue eyes and smiled. If this was the way he always went about making her feel better, she would be willing to get into more arguments to be with the man she loved.

"Are you ok now?" Doug asked with a grin.

"Yes, better now with you."

Doug smiled. "It doesn't matter what anyone says Lisa: I love you."

"I love you too, Doug."

Chapter 20

It was the first weekend in December. Lisa was in the kitchen brewing water for hot chocolate. Since Doug loved hot chocolate for heart to heart talks, she brought both mugs into the living room and sat down next to him.

Doug was watching TV. He stopped and looked up when she offered a mug to him. He pulled off his glasses and turned the sound down.

He knew that Lisa's soccer team had a tournament in Birmingham, Alabama the next weekend. They really never discussed the details and it was coming up soon, and he wondered if the hot chocolate was to talk about that. He'd been pretty vocal on his opinion of her current traveling plans. "Lisa, I don't want you to travel alone."

Lisa sat next to Doug and placed her mug on the coffee table. She was upset with Doug's chauvinistic behavior. She traveled anywhere she wanted before she met him and he wasn't going to stop her now. "Doug, I traveled anywhere and everywhere before I met you. You're not stopping me now."

"I don't intend to stop you, Lisa. I plan to go with you. It's not the same as before. You're pregnant now, and we're together."

"This is no different than any other drive to a soccer field."

"Yes it is Lisa. That's at least two hours away and overnight in Alabama. I'm going with you," he said adamantly.

"Doug, we aren't married yet and you can't stay with me. I'll have a couple of unescorted teens there."

"I'll stay somewhere else."

She crossed her arms, not liking how unreasonable he was being about this. "Since when did this become a dictatorship? You're telling me what to eat, you're driving me to work, and you're at my soccer practice. It was one thing when we unintentionally ran into each other, but now I can't get a few minutes to myself."

"You will get time to yourself but not now. We've got a lot going on and you can't do this by yourself. We're doing this together." Doug said in a deep southern drawl that grew sharper and louder with each word he stated. It struck a nerve with Lisa.

Lisa's voice got loud as she jumped off the couch to face him as he was seated. "We agreed that we were still going to be our own people, Doug, do our own things. I don't know if we can make it if we can't hold to that promise."

Doug stood up as she was talking, opened his arms and wrapped her in them as she squirmed to get away from him. Clasping her securely, he said, "I have an idea, I can stay with a college friend. This way your families are not upset and yes we'll make it."

Lisa thought over Doug's suggestion. She was used to handling the soccer team with assistance from the parents. She never had a boyfriend in the past that was interested in her activities enough to come or assist. She rethought his offer to come along.

"I guess that would be okay. You can come with me to the games and go to your friend's afterwards."

"Perfect. I'll make the arrangements"

***

Doug and Lisa took off early on Friday morning so they would have time for Lisa to meet his college friend and his family before the team got there. They arrived at Kevin's home and were welcomed at the door by him and his wife.

"You must be Lisa! Please come in." Kevin shook Doug's hand and smiled at Lisa. Doug made the rest of the introductions.

"Lisa, I want you to meet Kevin and his wife Amanda."

Amanda hugged Lisa.

"Come in and meet the kids," Amanda said.

Two children came running to the door full speed. Amanda yelled to them to "Slow down. We have guests." She smiled back at Lisa and Lisa grinned at the exasperated expression on the mother's face. "This is Colter. He's my ten-year old running back, and this is Shane. Shane wants to be a super hero. He's seven."

Lisa followed Amanda further into the house while Doug and Kevin walked out to the deck. Kevin opened a smoker full of ribs. The whiff of cedar wood filled the air. He stuck a fork into the meat and turned several pieces. He offered Doug a brew. "What happened? You get bored with white women."

Doug laughed. "There's a story behind our meeting."

"Yeah? What's the story? Did the both of you get stranded on a desert island and she was the only woman available? I heard black women were exotic."

Doug laughed. "The short story is I approached her on a bet that I lost. The long version is that she's been with me ever since we met."

"So do we have a slave master relationship going on here? You must be the slave because ever since I've known you, you were the master in every relationship"

Doug forced a smile on his lips. "Look, I know you're joking an all, but I really love Lisa. Fate brought us together and there are enough bigots coming out of the woodwork to break us up that I don't need my good friend acting the same way."

"I didn't mean...of course I'm happy for you, man. She seems like a great woman."

"She really is."

Kevin clapped Doug on the shoulder, and Doug did his best to push the awkward moment aside.

"So the wedding is in February—"

"Yep"

"Wouldn't miss it, man."

***

Lisa and Amanda toured the house and the kids followed their mother narrating over her and Lisa's conversation.

"I understand that you and Doug are getting married?"

"The wedding will be in February. We would love for you to come." Lisa said.

"You're marrying the guy downstairs!" Colter's eyes got really wide and his mouth fell open.

Lisa smiled indulgently. "Yes, Doug and I are getting married. Do you play sports?"

Colter smiled as he was now the center of attention, "I play baseball and football. My brother plays soccer."

Lisa said to Colter, "I coach soccer. That's why we're here this weekend."

Shane spoke up. "Really, I love soccer. Let me show you my room."

Lisa followed Shane to his room and saw all of his pictures.

Lisa asked, "Do you want to come and watch my girls play this weekend?"

Shane answered, "Sure! Mom can we go?"

Amanda laughed, "We'll check with your father."

The tour ended in the kitchen.

Amanda prepared a late lunch while Doug and Kevin came in bringing the meat from the smoker. She made baked beans, green beans, corn, cornbread to go along with the smoked chicken and ribs.

Lisa was thankful that Kevin and Amanda ate regular food as she wasn't up for venison this evening.

"Go Auburn!" Kevin said.

"Go tigers!" Doug said with a smile.

Lisa looked over at Doug and realized that he must really be a good attorney. He rooted for the bulldogs at her parents' house and was now rooting for the tigers. Doug smiled and winked at her.

"Are you an Auburn or Alabama fan?" Kevin asked Lisa.

"I went to UNC so I'm ACC not SEC. I have no dawg or tiger in the fight. I played soccer. My family are UGA fans."

Kevin nodded and Amanda spoke up. "I went to Ole Miss. I've got some great memories. I still keep up with my sorority sisters."

"Soccer was my sorority. I didn't have time for anything else." Lisa glanced at her watch and realized that it was getting late. Doug took the hint and backed away from the table. Lisa made her apologies. "My soccer players will be arriving at the hotel soon so I'll need to go."

"No problem, Lisa. It was so great getting to meet you," Amanda said, giving her a hug in farewell.

Doug smiled, "I'll be back after I drop Lisa off at the hotel."

Chapter 21

Doug rose early Saturday to arrive at the hotel. He walked into the lobby and spotted Lisa and her team eating breakfast. He smiled, watching as she managed the parents, corralled the girls, kept everyone on track and stayed calm. He knew not to approach her while she was giving the girls her instructions and expectations to the game.

Lisa acknowledged his presence when their eyes met momentarily. She released the girls a few minutes later. Doug was talking to Miranda, who was a parent from the team, when Lisa approached him.

"Are you ready to go?"

"I am."

"April and Corky are riding with us."

"I'll make room for them." Doug quickly left so he could make room in the car for the soccer players. They arrived just as he was finishing up.

April and Corky greeted him, "Hi Mr. Doug."

"Hello ladies."

The girls climbed into Doug's backseat to ride to the field. They were chatting with each other on the way to the game while Lisa was busy giving Doug the directions.

Corky interrupted. "Mr. Doug, do you play sports?"

He responded. "Tennis. I played soccer in school though."

April asked, "How did you meet our coach?"

Doug and Lisa proceeded to tell the story together. By the time they were finished, they were at the field. Doug and the players set everything up and he excused himself so that Lisa could coach her team.

The game got underway and Doug sat with the parents from Lisa's team. They were accustomed to seeing Doug at almost every game.

By halftime, neither team scored a goal.

During the second half, Corky suffered a hard tackle and went down on the field. Lisa was waved to come get her and Doug rushed to the field to assist. Doug and another player walked Corky off the grass and Doug attended to the girl's ankle while Lisa made the substitution. The referee continued the game and Lisa turned to Doug on the sideline. "How's she doing?"

Doug lifted his head to give Lisa a response.

"I think it's a bad bruise but not a sprain. I'm waiting to see if there's any swelling. I'm going to wait a few minutes before I ask her to stand up and put weight on it."

"Okay. Keep me informed, okay."

"No problem, Lisa."

Lisa turned back to the game.

Doug helped Corky to stand and she was able to put some weight on her foot. He asked her to sit back down so he could continue to put ice on it.

"I thought you were a lawyer. How do you know so much about medicine?" Corky asked.

Doug answered, "I actually went to medical school and decided not to practice. I went to law school after that."

"You went to Law school and Medical school? You must really be smart." Corky was impressed.

Doug responded, "No ma'am, just indecisive," And Corky laughed.

Corky jumped up Doug caught her when she screamed in pain at her sudden movement in response to the cheering from the crowd. He turned to look at the field. Several members of Lisa's team were in a huddle jumping up and down.

"What happened?" he asked Corky.

"April just scored. I forgot about my ankle. That hurt to jump on it."

Twenty minutes later, team had their first victory of the weekend.

The next game was in five hours and the team needed to get rest in between games. They decided to eat at a local mall so they could rest in between games. Corky was able to walk but she did so gingerly.

Doug and Lisa stayed with the parents as the girls walked around the mall. Lisa gave them a time to return and proceeded to the bathroom. One of the mothers came with her.

Vanessa said, "Doug doesn't leave your side. He's at all of the practices and all of the games. He's very attentive to you. You're very lucky."

"Thank you. He wants to make sure I don't lift anything heavy."

Vanessa asked, "Why? Are you pregnant?"

Lisa turned to the mother to respond. "Yes, I am. I didn't want to disclose that to the girls because I didn't want to set a bad example. I think most of them have guessed it but that isn't the reason why we're getting married. This happened the night we got engaged."

Vanessa said, "Well congratulations are in order for both pieces of news." Vanessa turned to the sink to wash her hands, easily changing topics now that the gossip was out of the way. "You do know that Tracy isn't happy with her daughters playing time. They're probably looking at another team next year."

"I understand. It's hard to be a goalie without a lot of playing time. We'll see what happens in the spring."

Chapter 22

Doug and Lisa arrived at the field for the second game.

After assisting Lisa with setting up the field, he walked over to the bench and sat next to a one of the parents.

"I'm Matt. Dana's dad. We hadn't been formally introduced."

"I'm Doug, Lisa's fiancée."

"Will she be coaching next year in the spring?"

"I'm sure she will." Doug answered confidently. "I'm not sure about the fall. That's her decision to make."

"I heard about the baby. Congratulations. Will she let us know in the spring? Some of the parents want to know. They're considering looking for another team if she isn't coaching."

"I'm sure she'll tell you all. I'll let her know your concerns."

The whistle blew and the game started. Doug watched Lisa carefully. She was not as active as she was in the first game. She took a seat and coached from the sidelines instead of her usual pace of walking up and down the sidelines. Doug knew that if he walked over to her during the game that she would be upset. Half-time was a no-no as well since she was giving instructions to her team. This didn't stop Doug from worrying about her health.

The girls won their second game 2–0. The parents and team were very happy. Doug rushed over to the sidelines and grabbed a drink for his fiancée. He pulled her to the side when he could break her free from the team.

"Lisa, Drink this. You're going down fast."

Lisa looked at Doug and knew he was right. She felt a little dizzy and everything became a little blurry. He noticed her swaying where she stood and rushed her to a seat. He gave her the sports drink and encouraged her to take small sips at a time. Dana noticed the coach was looked flushed and brought over a cool towel and Doug applied it to the back of her neck.

"Lisa, look at me. How are you feeling?'

"A little faint, Doug. Thanks for taking care of me. I'm really glad you're here."

"Take a few minutes and we'll get you to the car. You have to rest. You overdid it today."

"Ok Doug."

After fifteen minutes, Lisa was coherent enough to walk to the car. Doug reclined the seat so she could lay back and relax. Vanessa was nearby and Doug talked briefly to her.

"I'm taking her back to the hotel to get some rest. I'll let you know how she's doing."

On the ride back to the hotel, Doug was silent about his concerns. Lisa was very strong willed and whatever he would say could cause a major argument. He wanted her to rest and take care of the baby, not get riled up about him telling her to take better care of herself.

"I know what you're going to say," Lisa sighed and rolled her head from side to side. Suddenly she felt nauseated. "Doug, pull over quick!"

Doug found a place to safely pull to the side of the road. Lisa got out of the car quickly and started throwing up the full contents of her stomach. Doug grabbed some towels and water and rushed to her side. When she was finished, he held her in his arms and encouraged her to take a few sips of water.

"Are you ok?"

"I'm fine, Doug. Just a little morning sickness. I've got to get back to the team. They need me."

"Lisa, I need you. Slow down. The team is fine. If you want to meet them later for dinner then you have to get some rest. Promise me that you'll do that."

"Doug"

"I'm not taking no for an answer. I want you to go directly to bed when we get back to the hotel. Let's go."

Back to the car and off to the hotel they went. Lisa was too fatigued to argue and Doug was really worried that Lisa was too stubborn to take it easy. He was going to have a hard time getting her to recognize that she had to make temporary life changes in order to accommodate their baby.

Some of the parents were waiting in the lobby when Lisa arrived with Doug. She walked over to the group with Doug following her lead.

"I'm going upstairs to rest for a while. We can meet here in the lobby around 7:00 p.m. to go out for dinner. I don't want the girls to eat too late."

The parents nodded and agreed with her statement. She looked at Doug and gave him a weak smile. "I'll see you for dinner. I'm going to rest."

Doug kissed Lisa on the cheek, "Take care, Lisa."

Chapter 23

Doug waited in the lobby while Lisa was resting for dinner. He brought his Wall Street Journal and started reading it. He was halfway through an article when he was interrupted by a familiar face from the team.

"I'm Ted. Maria's dad. May I join you?"

As Doug lowered his paper he motioned for Ted to sit.

"So when's the wedding?"

"Early February"

"Is Lisa coaching next year?"

Doug noticed that this was the second time this question had come up. It must be a very important to the parents to know. "Did you ask her?"

"No, we didn't know if you would allow her to coach with the baby coming."

Doug's eyes sparkled as he reflected on Ted's response. They hadn't discussed Lisa's plans on coaching after the arrival of the baby. He realized that this would be a very important conversation to have. Lisa would have to make time for the baby along with her other activities. What would she have to give up? "We're discussing it. She'll let you know her decision when the time comes."

A few minutes later, Doug spotted Lisa coming off the elevator as well as a man approaching her. Doug excused himself to make his way over to Lisa to see if she needed his assistance.

Lisa was startled by the man who approached her. He was an African American male and apparently wanted Lisa to give him directions to a local restaurant. By this time Doug was standing right behind Lisa.

The man asked Lisa, "Are you with him?"

Lisa turned her head to look at Doug, "Yes sir, I am."

"Dang sistah, I see how it is. I'm gonna leave you with that." The man walked away.

***

The team arrived at the Chili's at 7:15 p.m. All of the players sat at one table and all of the parents sat with Lisa and Doug at another. The waitress was particularly attentive to Doug. Doug didn't take notice but Lisa did.

She whispered to him, "Our waitress is flirting with you."

"I hadn't noticed," he said.

The waitress came back several times to see if the group needed anything else. Lisa watched the waitress return to the kitchen. She was giggling with two other waitresses. Lisa just shook her head.

Ted said, "Lisa, I think the waitress likes Doug. You better be careful."

Lisa responded, "Everything is ok. Doug doesn't want to be left in Alabama." Everyone at the table laughed including Doug.

"Lisa is not kidding; she would leave me here. I would have to bum a ride home."

Vanessa asked, "How the wedding are plans coming along?"

"My mother, my sister, and Doug are handling all of the details. I have been instructed to show up in my gown."

"I don't want Lisa stressed out, she has enough to worry about."

The waitress returned to check on the table. Lisa decided to have a little fun.

"Did you know that he was getting married?"

The waitress looked a little disappointed but managed to say congratulations. The parents watched incredulously.

"Well, where is your lucky bride?"

"She's sitting right next to me." Doug pointed to Lisa.

Lisa gave the woman a big smile.

Dinner wrapped up and the players went to their rooms for the night. It was a warm and breezy night.

Doug asked Lisa to take a brief walk with him.

"Lisa, you gave me quite a scare earlier today. I really want you to take better care of yourself."

"Doug, I'm fine. You're overreacting." Lisa was exasperated by his overbearing behavior but somehow knew that he was right. Her body was adjusting to being pregnant and she wanted to continue her activities as if she didn't have to make any changes.

"I'm not, Lisa. Will you just please trust me? I don't want anything to happen to you."

"It's not a big deal. Women get pregnant all the time. I'll be fine."

"Lisa, this isn't a soccer game. You don't just fall down and get up. I'm insisting that you slow down and take better care of yourself."

Doug's tone turned deep and sharp which sparked Lisa's anger. "What are you saying? Are you telling me to give up coaching? Because if you are, we're going to have a problem, Doug!" Lisa shouted.

"What are we going to do when the baby is here, Lisa? You're going to have to be a mother first. Are you really trying to say that your team is more important than your baby? Already the parents are asking me about your plans for next year's soccer season. Lisa, you can't commit to anything long term until the baby gets here."

"Are you kidding me? We're going to argue about this now. I've got a game to coach and hopefully two more tomorrow." She threw up her hands and stepped away from him, shaking her head. "Just go to Kevin's house. I'll see you in the morning."

"Lisa, don't—"

"Night, Doug." She brushed past Doug and stormed into the hotel.

Doug stood motionless, speechless as he tried to make sense of their conversation.

***

Lisa went to her hotel room to check on the girls that were staying with her. They were fast asleep so she went back downstairs to the lobby for a few minutes to think about her last conversation with Doug.

She called a former soccer teammate, Courtney, needing to talk to someone about her domineering male.

"He sounds like he's very attentive to you. What's wrong with that?"

"Courtney, I like my independence. My life is moving too fast."

"Not your life, Lisa, you. You're moving too fast, and right now, you need to slow down. It's late. You're pregnant and emotional. You have big games to coach tomorrow and you need some rest. I know you're upset right now, but he loves you, and he cares, like, a lot."

Lisa laughed a little, hating the couple of tears that managed to fall down her cheek at her friend's words.

"Let it go for now and get some sleep" Courtney paused on the line, "Besides, I gotta get off the phone before I get in trouble with Doug and I haven't even met him yet!"

Lisa laughed as she hung up the phone.

Courtney was one of her best friends and knew how to show her the lighter side of life.

She was really glad she called her this evening.

She took a deep breath, and headed back to her room for some sleep.

Chapter 24

Doug slept restlessly that night thinking about his argument with Lisa. The same fiery nature that attracted him to her would also be the one thing that could tear them apart. Lisa was determined to keep the constant pace and not allow herself to truly connect with the major changes her body was going through. Somehow he had to get her to slow down.

Lisa wasn't able to sleep well either. She was upset with Doug for being too demanding and yet he cared so much about her wellbeing that he tried not to interfere with her wishes. When she looked at the clock, it was 3:00 a.m. Before she realized it, she had her cell phone in hand and was dialing.

Doug heard his phone ringing. It startled him at first. He turned on the lamp and scrambled over the nightstand to grab his phone from the charger. He recognized the number and immediately thought something was wrong.

"Lisa, are you ok?" Doug sat up straight and rubbed the back of his head. He started looking for his clothes to come to her rescue.

"I'm fine, Doug. I'm sorry for yelling at you. I'm not used to this pregnancy thing."

"I know. I'm not either," he said dryly.

"Doug!" she exclaimed in a half whisper-shout.

140

"I'm joking Lisa. Take it easy. You're going through a few hormonal changes. All of this is normal."

"How would you know? Well never mind. I forgot about the med school thing. I'm expecting you to act like my fiancé and not my doctor."

"I know. I can't help it. Please slow down and take care of our baby. I don't want anything to happen to you."

Lisa leaned back in her bed. "It's just all so fast, you know? I guess I say that a lot, but…"

"I'm here. We're doing this together."

"I'm soooo tired. This is so much."

"You can't do this alone and I won't let you. Just listen to me. I'm not going to tell you anything that will be harmful to you."

"No more tonight. I'll talk to you in the morning. Goodnight."

"Good night Lisa."

Chapter 25

Doug arrived early Sunday morning to take Lisa to the game. She was having breakfast with her team and had an empty seat next to her. She looked up and waived to Doug as she saw him enter the lobby. He kissed her on the cheek and sat right beside her.

The girls were now used to coach receiving affection from her fiancé. They still giggled a little and Lisa was slightly embarrassed but smiled all the same.

All was right in her world with Doug.

***

The morning soccer game was successful.

The team won their bracket and were scheduled to play the championship game at 2:00 p.m. Kevin and his family were able to make the championship game and they sat with Doug. There was no score in the first half so Kevin and Doug took a walk at half time.

"I noticed that you don't like to leave Lisa. You're always by her side."

"I just don't want anything to happen to her."

"Like what happened to Tiffany?"

Doug took a deep breath as he reflected on his relationship with Tiffany. He met her while they both were taking a biology class in college. As they fostered their friendship, they discovered that they both aspired to become doctors. Doug's passion was pediatrics and Tiffany aspired to practice obstetrics. Tiffany and Doug planned to get married after medical school and have a house full of children. They dated for about a year when the car accident happened. She was killed along with his parents.

"I have to be there for Lisa. I couldn't be there for Tiffany. I never got to say goodbye." Doug was very solemn.

"What happened to Tiffany won't happen to Lisa. You have to have faith that the two of you will be together for a long time."

"I can't help it. I have to be sure."

"I'm still surprised that you're getting married, Doug. I've never seen you this committed."

"I don't know what I'd do without Lisa."

The men returned to the game now in progress.

Lisa's team was up by one goal. When the final whistle blew, her team claimed the championship title and the victory celebration began.

Chapter 26

Lisa worked late into the day before running to her doctor's appointment. Doug had set the appointment to ensure Lisa was taking the right vitamins for the pregnancy. Prescription in hand, she left the office to head to the drugstore not far from the doctor's office.

As Lisa parked her car, her cell phone rang. She searched through her purse and finally found it.

Missed call from Doug.

"Oh, what does he want now?" She said to herself. "He's worse than my mother worrying about me and this pregnancy."

She sighed and dialed him back.

"Yes, Doug?" She said when the phone clicked.

"How was your appointment?"

"Fine, Doug. I have to come back next month. Don't you have work to do?"

"I won't keep you, Lisa. Did he give you any prescriptions?"

"Yes. I have to go. I'm at the pharmacy. I'll see you this evening."

Exasperated, Lisa threw the phone back into her purse and marched into the store. As she approached the pharmacy, the pharmacist looked familiar. She had a white lab coat on and dark red hair. The pharmacist was talking to a customer in a whiny, nasally tone. Lisa thought back to the week she was at Doug's house and he had an unexpected visitor.

Lisa was at the cash register when the pharmacist turned towards her. The name tag read: "Debbie." Lisa finally made the connection and backed away from the counter to make her medicinal purchases elsewhere but not before the pharmacist called out to her.

"Miss? May I assist you?"

"I'm taking my prescription elsewhere." Lisa responded as she turned to walk down the aisle and out of the store.

She hurried, but the pharmacist reached her before she got to the door.

"Aren't you Doug Bader's maid?"

Lisa frowned and her nose flared. She felt a sudden rush of sweat beads popping all over her face. She snarled in a low and angry voice. "No, I'm not his maid, I am his fiancée."

"Humph, no woman has caught Doug Bader. You're a maid in love with her boss."

"Get out of my way and get back to work before I call your manager and you won't have a job." Lisa shouted. "I'll be taking this matter up with my attorney. I think you know who he is."

Debbie brushed past Lisa storming back to the pharmacy. Lisa walked out the door and almost pulled the handle off the car door forgetting that she needed to put her key in first.

She drove home angry, and forgot to stop at another store for her drugs.

"Stupid hormones."

***

Doug looked at his cell phone and had two incoming calls. He recognized Debbie's number and allowed it to roll into voicemail. The second call was from Lisa. Doug clicked over and wasn't expecting what he heard.

"Doug, if I ever see that woman again…"

As Lisa was still shouting while Doug tried to get her to listen to him. "Lisa calm down. What's going on?"

"Debbie!" Lisa proceeded to tell Doug about the incident with anger in her voice and talking really fast. Doug still tried to interject but gave up realizing that she needed to vent. When she calmed down, Doug carefully started the conversation.

"Are you all right?"

"Yes I'm fine."

"I need you to stay calm. I don't want you upset. You could lose our baby. I want you to come home and I'll meet you there."

"No, I'm not coming home I'm going to the movies with my sister."

Doug exhaled through the phone not sure what to offer that wouldn't set off more anger. "Home after the movie and make sure you get your prescription."

"Are you telling me what to do again? I'll stay out as late as I want to…" Doug pulled the phone from his ear wishing he hadn't said that. Waiting for a pause that eventually came, he gently reminded her of his evening plans. "I'm getting measured for my tux. I'll cut the evening short if you want me to do so."

Lisa sighed, "No just go and get that done. I'll be fine. Lisa hung up on him, and Doug sat stoically staring at the blank screen on his phone.

It was the hormones, he knew, but she was angry, and he couldn't blame her.

Chapter 27

Doug, Greg, Harold, Todd, and Todd's son, Rhett, the ring bearer, were meeting at the local mall to get measured for tuxedos. Although Doug and Todd had cross words, they made up in their own way so Todd and his family could participate in the big day. Bruce had already sent his measurements to the store and would pick up his tuxedo when he arrived in town.

Doug greeted Harold and Greg when they arrived and discussed dinner plans while they waited for Todd and Rhett.

Todd and Rhett arrived out of breath. Doug put his arm around Rhett's shoulder in camaraderie.

Todd said, "Sorry I'm late. The traffic was bad. I'm ready for my part."

Doug extended his hand to his brother, "I'm glad both of you made it. Let's go and get measured."

He ushered his nephew into the shop to get fit for their tuxes and his groomsmen followed behind him. Doug had selected his tuxedo a few weeks ago but still needed to get his final measurements down.

Greg chuckled as Doug growled at the pinch of a pin in his leg. "I bet Lisa's been stressed planning a wedding and being pregnant. How many times has she yelled at you?"

Doug laughed. "How do you know that she's stressed?"

"She's a sistah, that's normal. Get used to it." Greg said jokingly. "I tried to warn you. Sistahs are tough."

"Well I wouldn't have Lisa any other way." Doug grinned and then hissed when another needle pricked him and the man sticking him told Doug to remain still. "Guess who tried to call me today?"

Greg laughed, "You mean you are starting to get calls again? It's too late now. Where was she a couple of months ago?"

"This one I would not have gone out with again. It was psycho Debbie."

Harold said, "You may have to get a restraining order on her. Do you think she knows that you are getting married?"

Doug answered "That was the phone call from Lisa. Lisa was in the drugstore where Debbie works and they got into an argument."

"Whoa," Greg said. "I'm surprised you're not at county picking Lisa up. A mad black pregnant woman is nothing to play with."

"I'm realizing that." Doug said with exasperation. "I may have to up my stock in Grey Goose." Greg held his hand up for a high five.

Doug snorted, "Do any of you have anyone single that you don't like? You could introduce her to them."

Harold replied, "I don't have anyone I hate that badly."

Todd answered, "I could introduce her to my neighbor. He just got divorced and needs a girlfriend."

"I take it that you don't like your neighbor."

Todd crossed his arms with a mean grin, "Nope."

Doug, Greg and Harold laughed. The men finished fitting for their tuxedos and decided on a sports bar for dinner. Todd and Rhett had to get home to Alice, so they said goodbye outside the tux shop and went their separate ways.

Greg drove them all to the restaurant and they ordered drinks after they are seated.

Doug was on his third vodka martini when their food arrived.

"You better slow down. If anything happens to you, Lisa will kill all of us," Harold said.

"It's fine, Harold."

Greg interjected, "I'm with Harold. You've got a baby on the way. Life's different for you now. If you want numbers four and five, you'll have to have it at home."

"Then Lisa would kill me." Doug said somberly. "That reminds me, I'll have to stock up on Peppermint schnapps."

Harold said "Imagine that, a lawyer trying to beat the system ."

"I need to call Lisa to see if she's made it home."

Greg said "I wouldn't do that if I were you. You've had a few unless you want her to yell at you. We'll be here for another hour. Let your food digest and the alcohol disappear."

"Yea, we can do that."

Greg changed the subject. "So is living with a sistah what you expected?"

"I don't know what I expected," Doug answered. "It's just like living with any other woman. She has lots of stuff, and is moody and stubborn. The only thing I haven't seen is the things with wings and that's because she's pregnant."

Harold asked, "Do you regret asking her to marry you?"

Doug smiled, "No. It was time and she's the one."

***

When Doug arrived home, he climbed the stairs to find his beauty sleeping in between loud snoring. He laughed as she had a slight snort as she gasped for air. Stripping down to his shorts, he climbed in beside her.

Doug stroked Lisa's arm and caressed her firm abdomen and swollen nipples. Lisa's deep sleep was now shallow and the snoring softened. He felt her hand search for the tip of his fingers placing them between her thighs.

"Someone's awake." Doug whispered.

"I am. I thought you'd call me before you left the restaurant."

"I was with Greg and Harold for dinner. We got lost in conversation."

"How many did you have?"

"What?"

"Doug. Don't play me. How many?"

"Lisa, why don't you get some rest?"

"No, Doug, how many? I'm following a strict diet that you designed. You have to follow it too."

"I'm not pregnant." He whispered sarcastically

"I am. How many?" she touted back at him.

"Three." Doug said reluctantly.

"Goodnight, Doug." Lisa shook her head and pulled away from Doug's touch. "Good night, Doug." She snuggled into the blankets and Doug laid back against his pillow.

Doug knew that his drinking would be a topic of discussion. Secretly he was glad that Greg stopped him from having more.

Chapter 28

It was 4:00 a.m. when Lisa woke up out of her sound sleep. Her stomach was queasy and her lower intestines were cramping. The nausea hit her hard and she jumped out of the bed and ran to the bathroom. Bending over the toilet bowl, she hurled the dinner from the night before.

The sounds woke Doug up quickly and he rushed to be by her side. He ran the water and soaked a towel in cold water. Lisa sat down in front of the bowl with her eyes watering.

Doug sat next to her and dabbed the damp towel against her hot face. She was still in a daze and blinked in silence as he whispered to her.

"Are you ok Lisa?"

She drew a shallow breath and looked into his eyes. "I'm going to kill you when this is over."

Doug smirked, "That's my girl. A fighter 'til the end. Do you realize that you're threatening an attorney?"

Lisa picked up her hands and buried her face in them. She knew she was still tired and needed more rest. She sighed and then she started sobbing.

"Lisa, stop. It's fine." Doug assisted her to her feet and enclosed her into his arms. He felt her tremble as she was trying to compose herself. He kissed the side of her cheek gently tasting the salty tears that streamed down her face.

She embraced him tightly taking deep breaths to compose herself.

They returned to the bed and snuggled for the rest of the night. Lisa's thoughts drifted far off into the distance wondering how she was going to handle all that was thrown at her in a matter of weeks. She had a lot to do over the holidays with shopping, work, doctors' appointments and a wedding. She was thankful to have a break from soccer to handle all of her other activities.

Doug glided his fingers across Lisa's swollen breasts and abdomen. He worried about her and her many activities. He insisted that she follow his diet and slow down for her health and the baby's health. He hoped that she would listen to him.

"Doug," she whispered, "I'm glad you're here," She managed a small smile, "but I'm still going to kill you."

Doug stopped stroking her arm and whispered back, "No you're not. My son needs his father."

"How do you know it's a boy? This could be your daughter."

Doug laughed. "It's a boy. We're in trouble if he's as stubborn as you are."

"I'm not stubborn."

"Get some sleep. We both have to go to work in the morning and have a long evening ahead of us."

Lisa turned to kiss Doug softly on the lips. "Goodnight."

Chapter 29

It was early evening when Doug and Lisa arrived at Tommy's Christmas Tree Farm. Doug borrowed his brother's pickup truck to have a way to bring it home. His father used to take the family to go pick out a tree after Thanksgiving.

Doug always wanted the biggest tree so he could put a lot of decorations on it.

Lisa's family was used to having an artificial tree. Her mom and dad would store the tree up in the attic until Christmas time came around again. Her dad would put the tree together and she would decorate it with her mom and Terri. This was her first year with her new fiancé and they were going to decorate the tree together.

Earlier in the week, Doug and Lisa decided to get new decorations so they could begin their life together with new traditions. The baby would bring even greater joy the next Christmas. As they walked the grounds looking for the perfect tree, they recognized someone they both knew.

"Hi Ms. Potts. How are you?" Lisa said. She hugged her and smiled.

Ms. Potts recognized Doug and smiled at the both of them. "I'm glad to see the both of you. I miss having you in the building, Lisa but I'm really happy that you found each other."

Doug smiled and hugged her too.

"Looking a little scruffy, Mr. Bader. I don't remember you having a beard and a moustache."

Doug laughed. "No time to shave. It's winter and it keeps my face warm."

"We haven't seen you since the move. We're getting married in February." Lisa said. "I'll send you an invite. I hope you can come."

"I'll be there. I'll get my son to take me."

After Ms. Potts left, Doug and Lisa selected a tree. It took a couple of men to load it in the truck.

Lisa watched the men's struggle wondering if they were coming to the house to help unload the tree too. "How are you getting the tree in the house, Doug?"

"I called Greg earlier and he'll meet us at home. I'll call him again and let him know we're on our way."

"Maybe you should call someone else too."

**

Greg was at the house when Doug and Lisa arrived. Greg and Doug struggled to angle the tree into the foyer while Lisa directed from inside the house.

The final destination was the living room, and with much laughter and not a few curse words, the men managed to get the tree standing though it lilted slightly to the right.

"How's it look?"

"Great," Lisa said, smiling at Doug as he came to hug her.

She yawned, "I'm sorry, Greg, I can't stay to entertain. I'm going upstairs to get some rest. It's been a long day."

Lisa hugged Greg and thanked him for coming. Greg looked over at Doug, raised his hands in surrender letting his friend know that he wasn't going into his territory. Doug nodded at Greg signaling that it was okay. Lisa quickly left the room.

Greg waited until she left and said, "What's she trying to do get me killed." He chuckled. "I remember what you did to the last brother that tried to talk to her."

Doug laughed. "Let's go to the den and have some drinks. She's going to be asleep for a while. We can catch up."

Doug fixed his usual vodka martini and Greg had a rum and coke. They relaxed on the couch, turned on the TV and began flipping through the channels to find something interesting. Doug paused when he saw a news flash of a young black male that was killed by police officers.

"You're going to have to worry about that if you have a son."

Doug looked at Greg with a curious expression. He didn't connect to what Greg was talking about. Why would he worry about his son and the police? He would have access to almost anything he wanted.

"By the look on your face, that's not something you considered. Your family will be black, Doug."

"I don't have a problem with it. White women are boring, Greg. You can have them." Doug winked at Greg as he tried to make light of the situation.

"Ah, that's cold. You date one sistah and give up your phone book. I'm not you, Doug. The sistahs can't have me."

"If you ever change your mind, that one upstairs is taken."

Greg got up, took Doug's glass and fixed a refill for the both of them. Doug gulped his down while Greg was getting resettled on the couch. "Nah man, she's too spicy for my taste. I like my woman to be a tall glass of milk with a lot of sugar."

"Are you bringing Bambi to my house on Christmas?"

"Hell naw! I'm bringing my momma. She would kick my ass. She specifically wants a black daughter-in-law. I hate to disappoint her but she's not getting one."

"Why does it bother your mom? She likes me."

"That's different. You're not her only son. She grew up in Jim Crow days. She thinks my career will take a nose dive if I bring a white woman along with me. She doesn't understand that times have changed."

"I still don't understand, Greg."

"You will. In your own way. You've hung around my family long enough to know the conversation. This time around you'll be living with it."

Doug remembered at some of the family gatherings the topics of discussion were mainly about other family members as well as the local news. They listened to R & B music, reminisced about old times, and prepared heavy meals for the holidays. He always enjoyed Greg's family because they were entertaining to watch. They were very vocal about their opinions, argued and made up just as quickly.

His family gatherings were on a much more serene level. They often ate turkey, wild game, mashed potatoes, corn, green beans and biscuit. His mother didn't believe in staying all day in the kitchen and prepared the lighter southern fare. Once his dad's business grew, his mother started making healthier family meals. She prepared lean meats and counted calories. She was overweight and slimmed down.

Their family conversations were always about the business. Doug read a lot of books so he always had something to contribute to the table conversation. His brother was usually quiet and observed the family conversation.

Ever since his parents died, well, conversations were even quieter, no matter what Aunt Mona tried to do to make them more interesting.

Doug stood up and grabbed Greg's glass for drink number three.

Greg held his hand palm up to stop Doug. "No more for me. I have to drive. No DUI's on this executive's salary. Too much money to throw away."

Doug chuckled, "Okay"

"I hate to cut this short but I'm heading out. Early day at work tomorrow. We'll catch up soon."

Doug walked Greg to the door and bid his friend goodnight. He stood in the foyer reflecting on the past few weeks. Ever since his engagement announcement, he'd talked about race more often than he ever thought he would. He pondered more over Greg's statement.

"Your family will be black"

Chapter 30

Doug worked late on Thursday evening. He wrapped up his call with Lisa letting her know that he would be home soon.

He was organizing his papers when Mark Steward approached the door.

"Doug, are you coming to the holiday party?"

"Yes, I plan to be there." Doug paused from shuffling his papers to look up as mark took a seat. He sat back in his chair waiting for the rest of the conversation to develop.

Mark usually didn't sit unless he had something to share.

"I just found out that Kim Parks is coming to the party, you know who she is don't you?"

"Yes, she's got her own clothing line, married to a rap mogul, former model…"

"That's the one."

Doug was perplexed as to why Mark would start a conversation about a celebrity. "Yes, I know who she is."

"Mr. Whitman's niece, Carol, plays tennis with her and she invited Kim to the party." Mark leaned forward in his seat. "Kim caught her husband with another man, Doug, and she's looking for the right attorney."

Doug's ears perked up.

Kim Parks would be a major client if she selected Doug's firm to represent her in the divorce. The publicity would put Whitman Stacks on the map.

"Make sure you bring Lisa tomorrow night. She's the right image for our firm."

"Lisa's not an attorney." Doug replied in a matter of fact tone of voice.

"C'mon Doug. If Kim sees all these old white farts in a suit, she's running out the door. Land this case Doug."

Doug nodded as he understood the meaning of Mark's message: Lisa was black, and that was all that mattered.

***

Friday evening, as Lisa and Doug were getting dressed for the holiday party for his firm, Lisa looked in the mirror and noticed the slight bulge of the baby she was carrying.

She'd shopped the weekend before to find a dress that would accommodate her changing figure and now wasn't sure she'd made the right choice.

Doug stopped to stare at Lisa. He walked over to her and wrapped his arms around her waist, kissing the side of her forehead while they looked at their reflection in the mirror.

He was accustomed to their contrast in skin tones. Lisa was still the stunning beauty that he met in a bar while he was out with his friends. The meaning to their chance encounters produced a new beginning for the both of them and a baby to seal their connection.

"Are you almost ready to go?" he whispered in her ear as he kissed her gently.

"I am," Lisa said as she squeezed his hands tightly around her abdomen. "And I'll be ready to lay in bed with my fiancé when we get back."

"I forgot to mention this, but Kim Parks will be at the party."

"Kim Parks!" she shouted. "Are you serious? I didn't know your firm handled celebrity clients."

"I can't talk about our client list but since she is going to be at the party, I thought I'd share that with you."

"Will I get to meet her? I love her clothing line."

Doug reflected on his conversation with Mark. Maybe Lisa wouldn't mind helping him with his career. Representing a celebrity would give him name recognition and possibly a way to start his own practice. "I'll make sure of it."

***

Doug and Lisa arrived at the party about an hour later. Doug introduced Lisa to several of the guests he was acquainted with. Lisa went to mingle with some of the other guests when Mark Steward called Doug for a private conversation.

"Carol is in the limo with Kim Parks. They'll be here in thirty minutes. You're the golden boy, Doug, when you land this case."

"I'll do my best." Doug winked at Mark.

Mark was pleased that Doug was on board. "Remember, you're our favorite couple. We love diversity at our firm."

Once Mark left Doug knew that it could be a disaster if Lisa found out the she was the black face of a firm that she didn't work for. The discussion of race between them would have to go deeper than their surface level discussions.

As Doug was still reflecting on his conversation with Mark, he felt a tap on his shoulder. It was Debbie, the pharmacist. She was the niece of a major client and an invited guest. Doug remembered Debbie's confrontation with Lisa and wanted to be rid of her.

"Hi Doug, you haven't returned any of my phone calls. Didn't your maid tell you that I came by?"

Doug was annoyed by her presence, "I won't be returning your phone calls. I'm getting married in a few weeks."

"You are? I hadn't heard that." Debbie said.

Lisa saw that psychopath pharmacist standing next to her man trying to talk to him. She moved quickly to stand right beside Doug and leaned her head against his shoulder holding his hand. Doug gave her hand a gentle squeeze, turned his head and pressed his lips against Lisa's.

Debbie's eyes widened at their display and frowned in total disgust at them. "You people are sick. Stick to blacks and whites. There's nothing wrong with your own people."

She stormed off leaving the couple to stare in shock at her venom.

"I can't believe she'd—"

"I don't know, Lisa, she's—"

"I should tear her hair out!"

"Lisa!"

She had to fight to take a deep breath and ignore the rage flaming inside her.

"Not here. She's not important. I'm showing off my beautiful fiancée" Lisa shrugged but let Doug pull her back into his arms. "It's almost time for dinner so we need to find our table."

Chapter 31

Doug and Lisa were seated at Mr. Whitman's table. It was very rare that Mr. Whitman sat with anyone at a function that wasn't a partner, so Doug was nervous and Lisa preened for the attention the bosses were showing her man.

Lisa looked at the name card next to her, excited to see that it was Kim Parks.

Kim arrived with Carol and the pair were chatting away as they seated themselves at the table. Lisa glanced around the room at the invited guests and realized that she and Kim were the only African American people there.

She suddenly understood why they were sitting with Mr. Whitman.

The firm needed another black face at the table and Doug was the only attorney that knew one.

"Ms. Parks? It's nice to meet you. I'm Lisa Dunbar, Doug Bader's fiancée."

Kim warmly smiled and said, "Call me Kim. Are you an attorney here?"

"Doug is a divorce attorney." She introduced him and Kim nodded her head and continued to smile.

"Nice choice sister."

Lisa laughed.

Doug pretended that he didn't hear what was said.

Mark, sitting to Doug's right, leaned close to whisper in his ear: "It looks good already. Lisa's doing a fine job for the firm."

***

After dinner wound down, Doug and Lisa mingled with other guests. Harold and Hannah came to greet the couple. The evening moved very quickly and usually they would have greeted each other earlier. Doug leaned into Lisa for a quick kiss when the pair approached them.

"I see you're at it again. I think the entire firm saw you kiss her," Harold said jokingly.

"It's nice to see you again, Lisa." Hannah said as she hugged Lisa. "I heard you were expecting. Congratulations."

"Thank you." Lisa said with a smile, pulling away from Hannah's hug to remove herself momentarily "I'll be back to talk to you in a minute. I'm going to the ladies' room."

"I'll go with you," Hannah said.

Hannah and Lisa both found free stalls.

Lisa was behind the bathroom door when she overheard two women come in and start a conversation.

The first woman said, "Can you believe that Doug brought his black fiancée to this event? Everyone is talking about it. Doug is going to ruin his career by marrying her."

The second woman replied, "I heard once you go black, you never go back. I never thought that he would actually marry her."

"When he brought her to dinner the first time and introduced her as his girlfriend, I thought Mr. Whitman's teeth were going to fall out."

"I can't believe he let Doug and his fiancée sit at his table."

The first woman said, "He's the only one that knows someone black. I heard Kim Parks wants a black attorney for her divorce but Mr. Whitman won't hire one."

The squeaking sound of the hinge on the door signaled the women were leaving. Lisa could still hear the sound of their voices as they exited the bathroom continuing to discuss Doug and blacks and black inferiority.

Lisa was too stunned to move. She didn't know whether to be angry or just forget what she heard. By the time she came out of the stall, Hannah was washing her hands and looked a little flushed.

"Are you okay, Lisa? I know you heard those women talking."

"I'm fine." Lisa said gritting her teeth. She knew that this was only the beginning of things that would be said behind her back and to her face about her marriage to Doug.

Chapter 32

Doug watched Lisa come from the restroom.

He made his way over to her. He sensed something was wrong. "Are you okay?"

"I'm just a little tired." Lisa's face tightened as she reminisced about the conversation in the bathroom. She stared at Doug wondering how much he knew about the evening and why they were there.

"We've stayed long enough to have made an appearance. I'm ready to go when you are."

"Thanks."

Lisa was silent on the way home. Doug imagined that she was tired and needed extra rest. She woke up when they approached the house.

"I'll make hot chocolate if you want it." Doug said.

"Sure, Doug."

Lisa and Doug decided to change first before having their late night hot chocolate. Lisa was still fuming from the events of the evening. She stood in front of the mirror as Doug unzipped her gown. She stopped him and turned to ask her question.

175

"Do you think your career is ruined by marrying me?"

Doug was stunned by her question. He responded quickly without any thought. "My life is ruined if I don't marry you. Why the question, Lisa?"

"No reason."

"Lisa, what's going on? Are you having second thoughts about this?"

Lisa turned around and looked deeply into Doug's blue eyes.

Doug could see that she was angry. "What's wrong? You looked upset earlier. What happened?"

"Why do you think we sat with Mr. Whitman?"

Doug was startled by her question. He'd almost gotten away with it. "To entertain Kim Parks."

"Did you know that she's looking for an attorney?"

Doug shrugged his shoulders, "Yes."

Lisa got angrier, "Did you know that Mr. Whitman won't hire black attorneys?"

"No, Lisa, I didn't. Where did you hear that?"

Although he knew that his firm handled elite clientele, he never thought about the race of his clients. Scanning back through his two years at the firm, he'd never had a black client or seen a black attorney.

Maybe Lisa was on to something.

"I just overheard a comment in the bathroom. Your firm is racist."

"Lisa, the firm is where I work and not who I am. We're in the south. Old prejudices die hard. Any firm I work for may practice the same racism."

"So you're going to continue to work in a racist firm?

"What do you want Lisa? We have expenses."

"And you can't work anywhere else to pay for those expenses?"

"Yes I can. Private practice is also an option."

"How much did you know about this evening?"

"Lisa, I found out Thursday evening that Kim Parks was coming. I was unaware that we would be sitting with Mr. Whitman or expected to entertain Kim."

"But you went along with it."

"Of course I did."

"And didn't tell me. How am I supposed to trust you?" she yelled. "You're supposed to clue me in."

"Look, calm down. I'm protecting you."

"No you're not. You're protecting yourself. Did you think that I wouldn't figure it out?"

"What do you want? An apology? How about sorry I fucked up?"

Lisa's frustration culminated into an outburst of tears. Doug pulled her tightly and allowed the tears to flow into his chest. She released Doug and sniffled through her voice.

"I'm still mad at you. Normally this stuff doesn't bring me to tears. I've cried more in the last three weeks than I've cried in the last three years. I don't know what's wrong with me."

"You're pregnant, Lisa. It's the hormones." He led her towards the bed, "Let's get some rest. We'll drink hot chocolate tomorrow. We've got a long day planned."

Chapter 33

Lisa was sleeping lightly when she smelled eggs cooking in the kitchen. The smell nauseated her stomach so her first stop was to the bathroom to let everything up from the night before. She washed her face, looked in the mirror and shook her head.

"I still can't believe I'm pregnant," she said to herself out loud. She brushed her teeth and went downstairs to see the full breakfast spread that Doug had on the table.

"I heard you in the bathroom. Sorry about the eggs."

"How did you know it was the eggs?"

'I'm really good at guessing what nauseates you. I won't give you any eggs. I have other food."

Doug prepared a plate for Lisa with fruit, yogurt and dry toast. Lisa was happy to eat something cool.

"Where are you going this morning?" Lisa asked.

"Christmas shopping with Greg. I'll be out for a while but you can reach me by cell."

What Lisa didn't know was that Doug was actually shopping for a Christmas present and a birthday present with Lisa's mother. Doug believed that this would give him a chance to get to know his future mother-in-law better and she would be able to help him pick out a gift that Lisa would like.

"Terri's coming over later. I'm getting my hair done this morning so I'll be leaving soon."

"Lisa, I meant to ask you, why it takes so long to get your hair done. Your last appointment was four hours. I thought I was going to need a search and rescue team to find you."

Lisa laughed. "I'm sorry Doug but that's one of the pitfalls of being a black woman. Depending on what service you want and how many people are in the shop, it can take a while."

"Are you sure you don't want to cancel and stay home. You look like you need more rest."

"I'm fine. I'm also beginning to believe you Doug. I've got to take it easy. I'll get some sleep under the dryer."

***

Doug had a stop before taking Ann shopping.

It was John Cascade's Art Gallery. Doug decided to commission a painting for Lisa's wedding present and was stopping by to talk to John about the details.

John was a friend of Doug's that he once in a while purchased art work from and donated to charity auctions. John's studio was starting to gain popularity among the working professionals who wanted art that was original but not so expensive that they would have to get a second mortgage on their home.

John greeted Doug at the door with a friendly smile and handshake. "What brings you by? You ran out with Lisa the last time you came to see me."

"I'm sorry about that. She and I had to talk."

"That's okay Doug, you're here now. What's new in your world?"

"Lisa and I are getting married. I want to give her a special wedding gift." John's eyebrows rose in disbelief.

"Lisa, the sistah? The one you left with? Are you serious? That must have been some talk. What did her family say?"

"They were expecting the news."

"Doug, I didn't know you dated sistahs."

Doug chuckled and blushed slightly. "Only Lisa. The wedding is in February."

"February! You don't waste any time do you."

Doug grinned and gave the rest of his news. "Lisa's expecting. We moved the wedding up."

"Doug, you are full of news. I thought you were the last confirmed bachelor. It took a sistah to get you to commit."

Doug smiled and changed the subject. "Lisa really loves your work. I have an idea what I want." Doug gave John a few pictures of Lisa that he borrowed from her photo albums.

John grinned. His deep dimple made a small cavern in his left cheek. "It's on the house, Doug. Consider this my gift to you."

"Thanks, I know she will love it. I've got to take Lisa's mom shopping."

An hour later, Doug arrived at the Dunbar home to pick up Ann.

Ann answered the door and Doug went down to say hello to Lisa's father in the den before leaving with Ann. "Hello Mr. Dave."

Dave shook the hand Doug extended. "Hi Doug. I hear you're brave enough to go shopping with my wife."

"I've been shopping with your daughter; it can't be any worse than that."

Dave laughed at Doug's assessment. "Probably right, son."

"Doug, are you ready to go?" Ann shouted.

"You better go. Can't keep the boss waiting," Dave said.

Doug winked at Dave and responded to Ann's call. "I'm ready."

***

Doug and Ann agreed to shop for maternity clothes for Lisa at the mall. They passed several stores before Ann stopped in front of a window that appeared to have a mustard colored urn.

"That's beautiful. I would love to have it in my living room."

Doug nodded and they continued to the maternity section of the department store. Doug was afraid to guess what size Lisa wore since her body changed some because of the pregnancy. He'd looked at the tags in her clothes to have an idea of where to start, but wasn't sure what to look for to accommodate her swelling belly. He was certainly glad Ann came along,

"May I help you, ma'am?" asked the young brunette store clerk. She was a petite size with dark brown eyes.

"Just browsing." Ann said.

After selecting a few items, Ann approached the register. After everything was rung up, the clerk gave Ann her total. Doug approached and waved to Ann signaling for her not to reach into her purse.

"I've got it, Mom." He said.

Ann looked at Doug and wasn't sure what to say. Since Doug and Lisa got engaged, she didn't know what she wanted him to call her. Ricky always called her "Ms. Anne." She wasn't sure she liked that, and mom felt oddly right coming out of this man's mouth.

She still didn't move but allowed Doug to complete the purchase with his platinum American Express credit card.

Doug grabbed the purchases and escorted Ann to the door.

More window shopping allowed them to learn a few things about each other. Doug found out that Ann loved candles, pottery and expensive purses.

Ann took this time to observe Doug's comfort level of shopping with her. He was very polite and patient. When Ann wanted to spend extra time in a store, he would either wait on a bench in the mall or shop in a separate section.

Doug called to check on Lisa while Ann was in a store looking at purses. "Still getting your hair done. How long have you been there?"

"Shut up Doug. Aren't you shopping with Greg? I'm enjoying my time to myself before coming home to you."

"I'm hurt Lisa. You'll have to make this up to me when I get home."

Lisa laughed, "I will."

"Bye, Lisa."

Ann walked up as soon as he hung up the phone.

"Are you ready for lunch?" Doug asked.

"Yes, I didn't realize that time has slipped away."

Doug smiled and led his mother-in-law-to-be from the mall and to his car.

They arrived at Imbrecia's Italian restaurant for a late lunch.

The hostess greeted them. "For one, two?" she asked.

"Two." Doug replied.

The waitress led them to a table.

Doug quickly pulled the chair out for Ann.

Once seated Doug began the conversation. "Thank you for suggesting the shopping trip."

"I had my motives. With everything moving so quickly, I need to know more about the man my daughter is marrying."

Doug smiled. He'd successfully evaded family interrogation for years. He knew that Ann ran a fair but firm household from the few times that he visited. Now was his turn to allow her mother to get to know him better.

"Ask away."

"If you haven't found out already, my daughter is self-sufficient. She doesn't need to depend on a man. We raised her that way."

Now he knew where she got the independent streak from, Doug thought to himself.

Her mother.

Getting a degree in law was the best move he ever made.

"How are you going to make my daughter happy?"

"Your daughter is happy. Stressed but happy."

The waitress interrupted to take their order.

"How's my daughter really doing with her pregnancy?"

"The morning sickness hasn't been fun for either one of us."

Ann put down her half empty glass of soda and remembered her daughter's stubborn nature. This would not be easy for Lisa because she would have to rely on others to help her with everything. The wedding, holidays, full-time job and new husband were only a portion of the things to do on her list in the upcoming year.

"Who's going to take care of the baby?"

"Mom, Lisa and I will discuss it." Doug placed his hands in his lap and squeezed his fingers tightly on his knees. Lisa's mom was getting excited and he had concerns of his own.

Ann frowned as she expected more of a committed answer. She pressed further to get a rise out of Doug. "What did your boss say about your engagement?"

"Congratulations," he leaned back in his chair, meeting her gaze. "Ms. Ann, I understand your concern. Lisa and I will work through everything."

He paused meeting Ann's eyes with a concerned look of his own. "Your family doesn't like me."

"What!" she said with disbelief. "Dave and I have treated you respectfully."

"Were you missing at Thanksgiving dinner? The reference to cracker was made numerous times and you weren't serving that for dinner."

Ann laughed.

Doug continued, "Ricky definitely doesn't like me. I don't think Lisa's aunts like me. I overheard some of the kitchen conversation too,"

"Oh, Doug, no, they like you, really," Ann said through her tears of laugher. "That's why they talked about you. You didn't listen long enough to hear them talk about the rest of the family."

"Am I always going to be the cracker in the family?" Doug asked. He knew that there would always be family gatherings and he didn't want to be uncomfortable.

"Sorry, Doug, but yes, yes you'll likely always be the Cracker. I have a tough family. Everyone has a label. Do I look like a Sha booboo to you?"

Doug removed his hands from his lap and started chuckling with tears running down his face.

"You better not repeat that or I'll have to pay a man named Guido to make you disappear."

"You'll have to wait in line. Lisa's got first dibs on my dead body."

"At least you got cracker as a nickname. It took years and people to die out to quit hearing that name."

"I get it. I must pay my dues."

Chapter 34

"Happy Birthday, Lisa!"

Lisa yawned, stretched and sleepily answered: "Thank you." She scurried out of bed to make a dash for the bathroom. When she returned there was a small box on the bed.

"For me, what do we have?" To her surprise there were hockey tickets. "Don't tell me. You're a closet redneck."

"No, closet Canadian. If you want my redneck side there's a wild game festival—"

"Stop. I want to keep the food I ate last night." She giggled. "I can't wait to go. I love hockey. How did you know?"

"It's close enough to soccer except with sticks, ice, puck, time outs and lots of fighting. Brutal sport. My next choice was a monster truck show, wrestling or drag racing. You aren't the opera type woman."

"No way, Doug. Not enough action." She paused and met his gaze, "Come shower with me while there's still room for both of us."

"Oh yea."

***

Quickly Doug slid out of the bed and raced to the shower door. Lisa followed his lead and was momentarily behind him. Twenty minutes later the pair were resting in the bed. Doug reached for Lisa and caressed her swollen breasts.

"You're giving me quite a workout."

"That's nothing," she said still panting. "After this baby is born, I'll really give you a workout."

"Promise." Doug said while he was grinning. "I believe we'll have to go away for that."

"You bet we will."

***

Doug and Lisa carpooled on the way to work. She received several calls from her family. Doug silenced the radio so she could receive her well wished. He glanced over at her waist which would soon be full due to her impending motherhood.

Everyone in the office knew that Lisa was engaged to Mona's nephew. When Lisa received flowers during the day for her birthday, everyone knew that they were form Doug. Lunch came soon and she spent it grabbing a quick bite to eat with Doug at a nearby cafeteria.

"Are you ready to go this evening?" When the waitress came by Doug ordered for them.

"I'll have the grilled tuna salad. She will have the lean chicken, broccoli—"

"I can order my own food." She said furiously. "I order what I want when you're not around."

Doug glanced up at the waitress. "Give us a minute please."

Once the waitress left, Doug address Lisa. "Lisa, just trust me. I have a vast amount of knowledge When it—"

"Then you carry this baby. I'm eating what I want when it's MY birthday."

"Alright Lisa, but you follow my diet the rest of the pregnancy and exercise. I don't want anything to happen to you."

The waitress returned. She wasn't sure who to ask about what they wanted to eat.

"I'm tired of this argument. Just finish ordering. I was going to order something similar. I've got to get back to the office."

Doug finished ordering and the waitress left the table. Doug's eyes sparkled and he flashed her his sexy boyish grin. He rose from the table and gently whispered as he kissed her ear. "I love you. Happy birthday."

Lisa sighed glancing at him with a twisted smile on her face. Her sandy blonde Adonis came with a price tag. The manipulating lawyer appeared and she was putty in his hands.

The food arrived and she began eating.

"Do you want to cut this for me in bite sized pieces?" Lisa said sarcastically.

Doug enjoyed her comeback.

"Oh Lisa, I would love to take care of that for you."

He reached with his fork and stabbed her chicken bringing the steak knife behind it to start cutting. Lisa chuckled and thought to herself: *I'm going to have to get some miles out of this and work his controlling nature to my advantage.*

***

Instead of fighting traffic, Doug and Lisa took the train to the hockey game. When they located their seats Lisa saw Corey. Both women like girls screamed when they saw each other and rushed to give and receive hugs.

"What are you doing here?" Lisa asked.

"Happy Birthday, Lisa. Doug sent me a couple of tickets. He wanted to surprise you for your birthday." Corey motioned to the man beside her, "Before we catch up, this is Ben, my boyfriend."

Ben had long dark hair in a ponytail. His beard was neatly trimmed. He was an average height man with a very lean body. He was holding Corey's hand.

"Pleasure to meet you." He said with a drawl.

"Texas" Doug said. "I'd know that accent anywhere."

Ben laughed as he shook Doug's hand. "Austin, to be specific. Not all southern accents sound alike. I can hear your drawl. Definitely Georgia."

The men laughed and Lisa smiled, linking her arm through Doug's so that he looked down at her. "Thank you for my present, Doug."

Once the game was over, Doug and Lisa took the train back to their car. Lisa was exhausted and immediately fell asleep on the drive home.

Chapter 35

Rev. Reginald Morris invited Doug to his Thursday night service for the youth group's career night. Doug had asked Greg and Lisa to come along with him the week prior. Greg readily accepted and met them at the church.

One of the congregation's members greeted them at the door. "Welcome to our service. Are you visitors?"

Doug answered, "We're here for the youth group's career night."

"Let me see if I can find Ikeda. Wait here and I'll be back."

Other members were still entering the church for the evening service and they greeted the trio as they were passing by. The petite woman returned with Ikeda in tow.

"I'll take you to the teen group, Doug. Why don't you all follow me?" Ikeda said kindly.

Ikeda took them to a classroom of about thirty teenagers. Among them was the youth minister who rose and greeted them at the door.

"Welcome to our youth group. I'm Pastor Sloan."

"I'm Doug Bader, this is my fiancée, Lisa Dunbar, and my good friend Greg Speaks." The pastor extended his hand to the trio. Doug had handouts prepared and gave them to the pastor.

"Pastor Sloan, I brought this information for your group to take home to read."

Pastor Sloan read over the handouts, "Impressive. Let me introduce you to the class."

Doug took the lead in introducing himself to the group. He spoke first and then took questions. Lisa and Greg took their turns speaking and took questions as well. The youth group was dismissed and the trio remained to talk to the pastor.

Pastor Sloan said, "I wanted to thank you for coming to our church today. Doug, I was curious as to how you knew so much about both fields of medicine and law?"

Doug answered, "I went to med school and law school. Don't ask me how I survived."

The pastor laughed. "And Lisa, I don't think you remember me. I went to high school with your sister, Terri."

Lisa looked him over. This was the man who used to write Terri love notes that were unsigned.

"I think I remember you now. How are things with you, Dee?"

"My calling is in the youth ministry and that keeps me busy. Give Terri my congratulations on her marriage to Ricky."

"I will."

Rev. Morris found the trio before they were about to leave. Rev. Morris extended his hand to thank the three of them for coming.

"Doug, it looks like I now owe you two favors. My wife and I would like for you and Lisa to come to dinner; Greg, you're welcome as well."

"We'll be happy to come by. It will have to be after the wedding. We're pretty busy with everything going on right now." Doug said.

"That's great. Have you found a church?" Rev. Morris asked.

"We're discussing it." Doug said as he heard Lisa's stomach start to growl.

"I'm hungry." She said. "Sorry to cut this short but I need to find something to eat soon." The trio bid farewell to the pastor.

"Greg, come with Lisa and I to dinner. I have to feed her fast. She is a little off my schedule."

Greg and Lisa laughed.

"I don't want to be the third wheel."

Lisa smiled and said, "You might as well come, Doug's orders."

The trio bid farewell to Rev. Morris and agreed to meet at Johnny's on the Side.

"Lisa, what's it feel like to take the most eligible bachelor in Atlanta off the market? I would have never thought that I would see the day that Doug got married."

Lisa and Doug both laughed.

"Doug and I both were talking about how fast everything happened. Besides planning for a wedding, I have prenatal visits to fit in as well as work."

The waitress interrupted them for drink orders. Doug took the lead in answering for Lisa.

"She'll have water with lemon and I will have a regular coke. Greg, do you know what you want?"

Greg was amazed at Doug. Lisa didn't have a chance to open her mouth.

"I'll have a rum and coke." The waitress left. Greg continued, "Lisa, are you going to be able to survive nine months of that?"

Lisa grinned. "Oh this is mild. Doug has a planner for every day for the next nine months."

Greg looked surprised and laughed. "You have her scheduled that tight?"

"Just about, I did leave a little room for flexibility." Doug slightly turned his jaw and winked at Lisa.

"I heard that it's your fault that I have him." Lisa said with a strained smile on her face.

Greg and Doug both laughed.

Greg said, "Oh not you too. I only bet him to talk to you and, as I recall, I won that bet. You shut him down. I told him that it wasn't easy to talk to a sistah."

"And what do you mean by that?" Lisa asked. Lisa stared at Greg waiting for him to dig himself into a further hole."

"Naw Lisa, You're not getting me into this argument. I'm happy for the both of you."

Doug changed the subject. "How did your meeting go with your fraternity?"

199

Greg drew a sigh of relief. Arguing with a pregnant woman with her man sitting next to her was not his cup of tea. "I found out we have some common friends."

"Who?" Doug asked.

"Carter Glass and Trent Davenport." Doug remembered both of the men very well for different reasons.

Lisa interjected, "Carter was in Terri's wedding. We met Trent at Doug's dinner with the partners." Doug slid his hand under the table and held Lisa's hand. Lisa gave it a light squeeze and changed the subject. "Are you native to Atlanta, Greg?"

"I lived in southwest Atlanta when I was a kid. My mother insisted that I go to private school for high school. That's where I met Doug. We've been friends ever since."

"Greg and I both ran track. Greg ran short distance and I ran cross-country. Greg taught me some things to increase my speed and I taught him endurance."

"Doug helped me out with math and science. My specialty was English and social studies." The waitress returned to take their order.

"Lisa will have the grilled salmon salad with a light vinaigrette dressing, no onions and I'll have the grilled chicken sandwich with French fries."

Greg shook his head and ordered. "I will have the bacon cheeseburger with French Fries."

The waitress left.

"At least you ordered enough food for me this time." She said as she squeezed Doug's hand tighter. Doug kissed her on her cheek.

Greg groaned. "We'll have to hurry up and eat so you both can get home for dessert."

Chapter 36

Doug woke up around 4:00 a.m. Christmas morning excited about his first of many Christmases with Lisa. Pressing his nose against her cheek he lightly brushed his lips against her skin. He didn't want to wake her but wanted to watch her as she was sleeping peacefully.

Doug's warm hands against her abdomen woke her from her slumber. Clasping her fingers into his, she exhaled, relaxing her entire body.

"Merry Christmas, Lisa."

"Merry Christmas, Doug."

Doug's moist lips placed small kisses against her neck. He desired to have breakfast in bed and Lisa was his main course. Lisa received his signal and warmly embraced her fiancé and father-to-be.

She stopped suddenly when she felt the familiar urgency of her early morning trip to the bathroom.

"I'll be right back, Doug."

Lisa slipped out of the bed and scurried to relieve the pressure in her kidneys. She returned with a little gift of her own in hand. Turning on the lamp, she slid into the bed handing Doug the small box. Doug kissed Lisa on the neck, scratching her with the bristles of his unshaven beard. Lisa squealed with delight pushing Doug way. Doug opened his present. Inside the box there were gold, silver and copper materials shaped like a T.

"Dental floss?" he asked.

They laughed.

Lisa loved his sense of humor. She anticipated that he would have something funny to say. "No, silly. It's a G-string."

"And what do I do with it?" he asked teasingly.

Doug loved the fact that Lisa was sexually expressive. She had no problems spicing up their love life. He knew that this gift was a teaser to their late night pleasure.

Lisa warmly smiled and responded. "If you take off your clothes, I'll show you where it goes."

"You promise?"

Lisa pulled Doug close rubbing her fingers against his warm, hairy chest. She fingered through his soft wavy hair and squeezed his arms, pulling him closer to her warm body.

While kissing Lisa, he quickly removed Lisa's pajamas. She caressed the inside of his thighs and his instant erection.

He removed his underwear.

Somehow the G-string never made it to Doug's body.

***

Doug and Lisa finally crawled out of bed to start their day around eight.

This was their first Christmas together. Getting up early allowed them to have time to exchange gifts privately before their family arrived.

Hand in hand, they walked down the stairs and sat by the tree. Doug gave Lisa a small box. Lisa made a guess that it was a piece of jewelry. She carefully tore off the holiday paper. Her eyes widened with excitement and she screamed.

"I love it, Doug!"

It was a silver bracelet that had an inscription on the back. "Love always, Doug,"

Lisa loved the personal gift.

"I'm glad you like it."

"I have a surprise of my own. Follow me."

As they approached the Movie room, she stopped Doug before he could move further.

"Close your eyes."

Doug smirked at her suggestion. "Alright, Lisa."

She held his hand and he followed five steps behind her with his eyes still closed. "Open them now."

He glanced across the room and noticed an old-fashioned popcorn maker like in the theater. Doug loved popcorn and hugged Lisa. He really appreciated his Christmas surprise.

"How did you get this in here? You shouldn't be lifting."

"I got my dad and his friend to bring it in yesterday while you were out."

"Thank you, Lisa. This is great for parties."

Chapter 37

Todd arrived with his family first. Mona carpooled with him and she was the first one in the door to greet Doug. Lisa was setting up the tables and greeted the family as they came in.

Alice brought in some prepared dishes and Lisa showed her where to put everything.

Doug and Todd went to the den. Doug circled around the bar and fixed his brother a sloe gin fizz. Doug's vodka tonic was on empty so he fixed another one.

Todd sipped his cocktail clinking the glass while observing his surroundings. "Where's your new relatives?"

"They're coming."

"I heard about black people and this CP time thing. What time did you tell them to be here?"

"Noon."

"You should have told them 10:00 a.m. and they might have made it on time. They probably won't show before 3:00p.m."

Doug nodded and remembered that Lisa's sister Terri was bringing that obnoxious husband of hers.

If Todd got drunk and Ricky got hateful, there could be a big family feud. He hoped that Ray would be in attendance because he would need an extra level headed man to break up any altercation.

An hour later, Lisa's relatives started to arrive. Ann and Dave arrived first bringing several gifts in hand. The rest of the family filtered in slowly after that. Only Terri and Ricky were missing as far as Doug could tell.

The Dunbar women started taking over the kitchen relegating Mona and Alice to the status of invited guests. Mona and Alice found a seat at the kitchen table and watched how the Dunbar women rapidly prepared dinner.

Lucille grabbed the roaster and moved it to the counter.

"That's mine." Alice said.

"What's in here?" Lucille asked curiously.

"Boar ribs." Lucille opened the lid and pulled one out. "I've never had these before." Crowding around to see the ribs, each of the Dunbar women took a bite from the one that Lucille passed around. Lucille grabbed a dish and transferred the meat.

Alice spoke up, "Can I help you with that?"

"I got this, honey."

Alice glanced over at Lisa with frustration in her eyes. Lisa caught her glare and shrugged with a smile, rolling her eyes at her families' exuberance.

"Alice, let's tour the house."

"I'm coming with you," Mona said.

They were soon out of range of the kitchen.

Lisa took the women to a guest room and closed the door slightly.

"I apologize for my aunts. They're used to taking command of the kitchen without any help. As you saw, I'm not in control of my kitchen either."

Alice nodded in frustration. "I'm used to preparing Christmas dinner or helping. It doesn't seem like Christmas if I'm not involved."

"I'll talk to my aunts. Maybe they'll listen to me."

They returned to the kitchen and the aunts were in full busy mode. The food table was now covered with all the dishes that were brought by the guests.

The three women looked at each other and decided it would be better to let the Dunbar's have this round. They'd drink lemonade while the other women did the work.

***

Odessa entertained the women in the kitchen by telling stories of Greg when he was a little boy. She annoyed Olivia so much that Olivia gave her several sous chef jobs to keep her busy.

"Have you heard from Terri?" Ann asked.

"No, I'll call her." Lisa said. She rushed upstairs where it was quiet to give her sister a call.

There was no answer and Lisa was concerned.

The doorbell rang and she rushed to answer it.

Terri and Ricky were standing there holding presents for the family.

"I thought we were going to have to send a search party for you. Where have you been? We expected you hours ago."

"We're here now." Ricky said. "We had to go by my mother's house."

Terri had a grim look on her face. With a strained smile, she said, "Merry Christmas."

Chapter 38

Doug and the men gathered in the movie room. His large screen TV was playing in the background though no one was paying attention. He introduced his brother to several of Lisa's family members.

Todd and Dave became friendly right away. Todd's background in construction was interesting to Dave who was a civil engineer for the state of Georgia.

"Dave I see you're a UGA fan."

Dave pulled his shirt from the center of his chest. "I'm a big fan. That's my alma mater. Did you go?"

"I couldn't. I took over the business when my parents died. Doug's the smart one."

"Running your own construction business takes a lot of talent. You work for yourself. The rest of us work for others. It seems to me that you're the smart one."

Todd nodded with appreciation. Since Doug was the genius of the family, Todd got very little attention for his accomplishments. He took it for granted that his abilities to run the business and provide for his family were just as important as being a lawyer.

Doug, Greg, and Ray were discussing the latest fashion trends for men. Because of Greg's status as a marketing executive, he was becoming more aware of the fashion trends. He traveled a lot and made presentations to customers as well as key personnel at his company. He was shaping his image so he could move further up the corporate ladder.

When Doug heard the doorbell, he hurried to the front of the house, hoping to spare Lisa the energy of trying to get there first. She still beat him to the door. Doug firmly shook Ricky's hand and stared into his eyes signaling that this was his territory and he didn't want trouble in his home. Ricky acknowledged his stare, nodded and returned the firm handshake.

"Did we miss dinner?" Ricky asked.

"We were waiting on you," Lisa answered tightly. "I'll let everyone know you're here and we'll eat soon."

Doug squeezed Lisa's shoulder. "I got this." He walked towards the kitchen. "Mom, Ricky and Terri are here."

Lisa smiled gratefully, watching Doug walk away before turning back in time to hear Ricky and Terri argue.

Ricky loudly whispered to Terri. "I don't know why your mother lets him call her mom. That's not his mother."

"Shut up, Ricky. I went to your family's house first and we said we were going to go there last."

"My mother was mad that you didn't eat."

"I don't care that your mother was upset that I didn't eat. Lisa, where's mom?"

Lisa and Terri disappeared into the kitchen leaving Ricky standing in the foyer. Doug returned and led him to where the men were gathered. It was a short stay because dinner was almost ready and would be served soon.

The family comes together around the table. Dave led the led the grace.

After grace was said, Doug pulled Lisa to the side and whispered in her ear. "Don't let Ricky sit next to my brother."

Lisa looked up and said "Ooh you're right. I'll get dad to take care of it."

Dave successfully interceded in redirecting Ricky from sitting next to Todd but he couldn't avoid them sitting directly across from each other. Two large tables were set Ann, Dave, Lucille, Olivia, Mona and Ray were seated in the kitchen and the rest of the family were seated in the dining room.

All were seated and settled in their places. Doug and Lisa watched anxiously to see if the fireworks with Ricky were going to extend to Doug's brother.

Ricky darted his eyes across the table to look for some seasoning. The salt was in front of Todd.

Ricky made his request. "Pass the salt."

"You mean the black pepper." Todd said sarcastically.

Lisa nudged Doug to pay attention to the conversation.

"Just give me the damn salt," Ricky said hastily.

"Get your own damn salt." Todd said with a touch of anger in his voice.

Ricky got up and grabbed the salt from in front of Todd and said in a low snarky voice, "I bet your ass is a Republican too."

"You're damn right I am."

Alice tugged Todd's sleeve.

Todd glanced over at her, "Leave me alone, Alice."

Ricky replied, "That's whacked. Republicans are racist. I bet you got a Confederate Flag too."

"I got the flag and my gun. Do you want to talk about this outside?" Todd and Ricky both moved forward as if to rise out of their chairs. Doug interjected in a loud tone of voice.

"No one's going outside. Both of you eat your dinner. It's Christmas. Respect my home."

***

After exchanging gifts, Todd's family was the first to prepare to leave. Doug looked for Lisa so she could bid them goodbye. He only found Ann cleaning up the kitchen with Lucille and Olivia.

"Mom, where's Lisa?" he asked.

"She's upstairs resting. I told her to lay down. Dinner took a lot out of her."

Up the stairs he went to check on Lisa. She was sound asleep and he chose not to wake her. He closed the door so she wouldn't be disturbed. He returned to his guests that were preparing to leave.

Todd was at the door saying his farewells. Alice and the kids were already in the car when Doug walked out with Todd.

Todd said, "That Ricky is a dick. I'm glad I don't have to put up with him."

"But Terri does. Feel sorry for her."

Todd nodded in agreement.

"Take care of Lisa. She looked really tired."

"I will."

***

After the remaining family members left, Doug went back upstairs to check on Lisa. She was beginning to rouse. She noticed that it was really dark outside and the house was quiet.

"Where's everyone?"

"Gone."

"Why didn't you wake me up to say goodbye?" Lisa yawned and sat up in the bed.

Doug hugged Lisa and gently caressed her cheek. "You needed your rest. You'll see everyone again soon."

ABOUT THE AUTHOR

MIA MAE LYNNE - has enjoyed writing from the time she was in grade school. She started a diary and wrote in the journal for seven years. She always knew that one day all of her creative ideas would come into fruition and writing has been her escape.

"The Chronicles of Fate" series was born in the metro Atlanta area allowing her to explore her creative side. The series was later renamed to "Southern Men Don't Fall In Love" with "Atlanta's Most Eligible Bachelor" as the first book in the series with many more to follow. She has really enjoyed writing the series and has embraced each of the characters as they have entrusted her with their stories to share with the world.

After discovering psychic and mediumship abilities, she became a student of spiritualism. She has newly begun this path and has explored the traditional areas of tarot, numerology, astrology and other related areas of interest in the metaphysical arts. She has received training from the Fellowship of the Spirit in New York as well as read numerous books and attended various classes to expand her knowledge.